Twisted Sisters

The Orion Circle Book 2

Kimber Leigh Wheaton

Published by
Sea Dragon Press

Twisted Sisters

Published by Sea Dragon Press

Copyright © Kimber Leigh Wheaton, 2015
ISBN: 978-0-9904026-6-4

Cover design by AM Design Studios
Layout by Guido Henkel

The author acknowledges the copyrighted or trademarked status and trademark owners of the products, characters, and services mentioned in this book. Any trademarks, service marks, product names, or named features are assumed to be the property of their respective owners, and are used only for reference: Keurig, Apple iPhone & Mac, Octane, *Anything Goes*, Ford Mustang, Jeep, Hyatt, *Indiana Jones, Richie Rich, Scooby Doo,* Diet Coke, Frisbee, *Spongebob Squarepants,* Avenged Sevenfold, *Ghostbusters, Supernatural,* Disney World, Cadillac Escalade, Motrin, Blu-Ray, Nintendo, Mario Kart, *X-Men, Star Trek,* Sony PlayStation, *American Horror Story, The Simpsons*

Printed in the U.S.A

*To everyone who has felt lost,
misunderstood, or forgotten.
And to everyone who has helped them
find their way home.*

*To my parents and my parents-in-law,
especially Joan.
I can always count on your support,
and that means the world to me.*

Table of Contents

~

Prologue - A Child's Toy 7

Chapter One - The Kiss 11

Chapter Two - Aftermath 19

Chapter Three - Rehearsal 30

Chapter Four - Sorority Sisters 36

Chapter Five - Chaos 44

Chapter Six - Three Nasty Ghosts 51

Chapter Seven - Rescue 58

Chapter Eight - Research 64

Chapter Nine - Morning 69

Chapter Ten - Circle Gossip 76

Chapter Eleven - Insidious 87

Chapter Twelve - Plans 96

Chapter Thirteen - Lesser of Evils 105

Chapter Fourteen - Angela 111

Chapter Fifteen - Back to the Lions' Den 123

Chapter Sixteen - Memories & Forgiveness 133

Chapter Seventeen - Retreat 144

Chapter Eighteen - Premonition   152
Chapter Nineteen - Danger   162
Chapter Twenty - Death Omen   172
Chapter Twenty-One - Trespassers   181
Chapter Twenty-Two - Ghastly Vision   192
Chapter Twenty-Three - Building Tensions   199
Chapter Twenty-Four - Tear Down that Wall   213
Chapter Twenty-Five - The Truth   229
Chapter Twenty-Six - Revelations   242

Prologue
A Child's Toy

Sunlight filtered through the sliding glass door, shining on the brown spirit board spread out on the antique oak table. A bright blue box emblazoned with the words *Fun for all Ages* sat beside it, along with an instruction sheet. One girl twirled the planchette with her fingers while watching her friend read the instructions aloud. A child's game bought at a toy store. What harm could it do? These two girls were about to find out that sometimes evil existed in the most innocent of packages.

"Okay, so it says to rest your fingers on that piece," Melissa said as she tossed the instruction sheet aside.

"If we put our fingers on it, then how do we know that we didn't move the thing?" Kendra asked, placing the planchette in the middle of the board.

"I don't know," Melissa said, rolling her dark eyes. "Did you want to try it or not?"

"Sure, why not." Kendra released a bored sigh that turned into a yawn. "Why are we up so damn early?"

"I wanted to get an early start." Melissa's shoulders scrunched up into a sheepish shrug. "Lots of time until dark, you know, in case…"

"It's a toy, Melissa," Kendra said with a snort of laughter.

"Maybe, maybe not."

"You're totally kidding, right?" Kendra stared at her friend from the corner of her eye.

Melissa kept a straight face for a few more seconds, then burst into laughter. "Fooled you!"

"Childish much?"

"Okay, just put your fingertips on this thingy." Melissa placed her fingers on the planchette before giving a pointed look to her friend.

"I feel kinda stupid," Kendra said as she placed her fingers on the opposite side of the planchette. "So, ah, if there are any spirits who want to communicate, we're here."

"Wow, that was dull." Melissa took a deep breath. "Spirits across the hazy veil. We call to you from beyond the pale."

"What was that?" Kendra asked, raising her brow.

"Just a little drama." Both girls stared at their hands which stayed unmoving. "I call to thee spirits for we are here. Any spirit nearby is welcome to appear."

The planchette began to vibrate and wiggle.

"Are you doing that?" Kendra asked in a shaky voice.

"No," Melissa whispered back. "Shh! It's starting to move."

"Is a spirit here with us?" Kendra called out to the empty room.

The planchette jumped a bit before sliding to the word, *yes*. But it didn't stop there. Before either girl could think to ask another question, it shot across the board, flying from letter to letter. Both Kendra and Melissa snatched their hands away from the shuddering, plastic pointer.

Kill, kill, kill. Over and over again.

"Who are you?" Melissa shrieked the question as an invisible wind blew her long hair around her body.

Amy.

"Amy?" The whipping air died with Kendra's question. Both girls trembled as the planchette moved to *yes*.

Tracy.

"There are two of you?" Melissa's face paled. Cabinet doors opened and slammed closed in rapid succession.

Renee, kill…

The planchette paused. Kendra took a breath to ask another question, but before the words reached her lips, the planchette spelled out a new word.

M…u…r…d…e…r.

"Murder?"

Goosebumps spread up Kendra's arms after she spoke. She hugged her arms around her body, trying to chase away the bitter chill. Dishes flew from the cabinets, smashing to the floor one after the other. Kendra pushed her chair from the table and fled the room. Drinking glasses from the cupboards flew across the room, hitting the wall where Kendra's head had been just moments before.

Us.

"You were murdered?" Melissa asked through a gasped breath. She clutched the edge of the table with white knuckles, too scared to move. Pieces of shattered pottery lifted from the floor on an invisible whirlwind, blowing around the terrified girl.

Yes, murder. Free, free, free.

1

The Kiss

~

KACIE

Restless, endless pacing. Nerves firing out of control. I wanted this, asked… no begged for this role, and now I'm regretting that choice. Why didn't the director mention that the lead characters had to kiss on stage? And not some chaste, sweet kiss. No, it has to be a long, passionate kiss. I stop and lean my head against the cool glass of the window overlooking the courtyard below. Students go on with their lives, oblivious to my turmoil. Little lemmings I wish I could stomp on to stop their stupid betting pool.

I was fine this morning. Daniel psyched me up last night, convinced me I—we could do this. But the moment I arrived at drama this morning, the entire class was abuzz with the news. We'd be rehearsing the kiss scene this afternoon. I can't even begin to imagine the crowd this rehearsal will attract. But I was still managing to hold it together until fourth period. That's when I caught wind of the betting pool.

Option number one: Kacie will throw herself at Daniel and dump Logan after one kiss.

Option number two: Kacie will run off the stage in a panic, unable to face Daniel.

Option number three: Logan will beat the crap out of Daniel or at least knock his teeth out.

Option number four: Kacie will be killed by the groupies before she can lay a lip on Daniel.

How can one kiss attract so much attention in the drama that is high school?

What about option five? Daniel and I act like professional actors and life continues on as normal. It's only been two months since I was almost possessed by a homicidal ghost. This is nothing compared to that. Yet even as I repeat that over and over in my head, my stomach rolls and I bite my lip hard enough to taste blood. Finally I give in to nerves and text Daniel.

Need help. Falling apart. Club room. Now.

Within moments my phone chimes with his answer. *On my way.*

Pushing away from the window, I glance around the dim club room. The Orion Circle is still new to me, though I've been a member for two months. Before the Circle, I was a scared physical medium who didn't know how to deal with the ghosts haunting her. The Orion Circle took me in, showed me I wasn't alone. They taught me how to use and control my abilities. Now I'm a paranormal hunter, a member of a group.

A wisp of memory floats through my mind, and I squash it down... but not quickly enough. The Fox-blood Demon almost possessed me, almost stole my body and soul two months ago. It's not something easily forgotten. Before his spirit, I never realized there were ghosts that powerful out there. While it scared me, it also firmed my resolve. That night we saved thirteen child spirits from a monstrous ghost. I watched them move on to... well with any luck a better place, smiles lighting their ghostly faces. Without the Orion Circle, I never would've succeeded. We are a team. I need them. They need me. It feels good to be needed, to be a part of something bigger than myself.

I wander over to the bookshelves lining the far wall. Nervous energy makes my hand shake as I run my finger along the spines. The Orion Circle's collection of paranormal books is a treasure trove. My finger stops on *American Urban Legends: Decoding the Paranormal,* and I yank it from the shelf. I'll need something tonight to occupy my mind no matter the outcome of rehearsal. As I'm shoving the book into my backpack, Daniel enters the club room.

"Hey, Cici," Daniel says with a tired smile. "How long have you been hiding up here?"

"Since I walked out of my chemistry class." My head falls back, and I stare at the ceiling like those boring tiles can provide insight into my foolish overreaction. "I overheard some girls whispering about the betting pool. When she noticed my interest, Karen handed over the paper outlining the options. I gathered my things and fled."

"Ouch." Daniel crosses the room to lean against the leather sofa. "So much for acting disinterested."

"Yeah, I panicked."

"It's just a kiss," Daniel says in a soft voice. "It's not the end of the world."

"Then why is everyone acting like it is?"

"Boredom, jealousy, who knows." He shrugs. "Does it matter? We'll create an option five where two professional actors kiss onstage without incident. It will make them all look foolish."

"I'm overreacting, huh?" I say with a sheepish grin. Daniel always manages to make me feel better.

"You ready to go to lunch?"

"Wait," I call out to his retreating form. "I've never kissed anyone on stage before."

"It's just me, Cici," he says without turning.

"It's just… rehearsals are hard. The house lights are up, and I can't lose myself in my character," I admit with a dry chuckle. "It's going to be Kacie Ramsey on that stage kissing Daniel Westin in front at least fifty witnesses."

"Yeah, I have the same problem." Daniel turns back to face me. "Did you want to practice first? Get the awkwardness out of the way?"

"Now?" He read my mind. "Yes, I think it would help."

Without a word he crosses the room to stand within inches of me, as close as he can get without touching. Unsure what to do or say, I stare at our feet. We're both wearing black hiking boots. They're kind of an Orion Circle staple.

"I had a crush on you last year." My hand flies to cover my mouth. I can't believe I just admitted that.

"I know," he replies, placing his finger under my chin to tilt my head up. All traces of the sarcastic Daniel I'm used to are gone. Instead I see vulnerability in his gray eyes. "Do you know why I never acted on it?"

"Acted on it?" I ask with a gasp. "You mean you liked me?"

"Oh, yeah," he replies, his lips turning up into a half-smile. "You are adorable with that dusting of freckles across your nose, those big, hazel eyes, and your panicked shyness that disappears the moment you hit the stage."

My breath catches in my throat. That entire time I pined for him, I had no idea he liked me too. I open my mouth to ask why he never acted on it but nothing comes out. My mind is wrenched back to that one moment in time when I made an ass of myself at the cast party. I tried to kiss him. He shot me down. Nicely. But still it hurt.

"My best friend had a major crush on you," he says, answering my unspoken question.

"Logan?"

He nods. "Logan certainly didn't come to all of those rehearsals to stare at me." Daniel's laughter is musical, and just like that the tension fades away.

"Logan liked me last year?" I ask, unable to stop the smile spreading across my face. "Why didn't he tell me?"

"He was too shy," Daniel replies with a snort. "And no amount of prodding on my part could convince him. You and Logan are meant to be together. You need each other, and as corny as this sounds, I think you complete each other. Certainly when it comes to psychic power. You and me? It would have been wild and passionate and burned up as fast as it started. I liked you far too much to lose you as a friend for the sake of a few kisses."

"Oh, Daniel." My eyes tear up from his frank admission. "I don't know what I'd do if I lost you as a friend." Just the thought makes my chest hurt.

"You won't, so don't even think about it," he replies. "Now shut up and kiss me."

His comment makes me laugh. "Thanks."

"For what?"

"Making me feel better," I say, pushing on his chest. "For always being there for me."

"Are you gonna kiss me or keep talking?"

"Why don't you take the lead?" I ask, stalling for time. *Can I do this?*

"It says in the script that you initiate the kiss," he says, shaking his head. "You think Mr. Holmes will allow me to lead this party?"

No. Mr. Holmes is one tough director. He would make me kiss Daniel hundreds of times if it wasn't done to his satisfaction. I don't know if he's a perfectionist, a sadist, or both. Taking a deep breath, I rest my hands on Daniel's chest. There's too much of a height difference. Even standing on my toes it's hard to reach past his chin. Why isn't he helping? Moving my hand to the nape of his neck, I guide his head down toward mine. Our lips meet in a chaste kiss. Just as I'm about to pull away and yell at him, he responds to the kiss. His lips move beneath mine for a few moments before he pulls away.

"Again," he says. "This time put your arms around my neck. Your character is an experienced night club singer and no virgin. Act like it. My character won't react immediately. That doesn't deter you, it just makes you bolder. Once my arms encircle you, count to five slowly, then pull away. Got it?"

I nod, determined to get this right. If we do it perfect the first time then Mr. Holmes won't have us repeat it. It will feel so good to blow those asshats and their stupid betting pool out of the water.

"How come not one of the options featured us acing the kiss at the rehearsal?"

"Because that would be no fun for the hecklers, jokers, and assholes who thrive on the suffering of others," he replies with a snort. "Now are you going to kiss me or not? I'm hungry and want to get to lunch before the line gets too long."

Once again I place both hands on Daniel's chest. Rising to my tiptoes, I snake my arms around his neck and press my lips to his. He responds much faster this time, wrapping his arms around my back. His lips are soft and pliant beneath mine. The kiss is very pleasant. My body likes it, and yet my mind is counting to five like I was told. Just before I pull back, I hear what sounds like the door clicking shut. When I turn to look, no one is there. Must have been my imagination.

"Now that was a kiss worthy of the stage," Daniel says with a brash grin. "Come on, let's get some lunch. I have a feeling rehearsal will go just fine."

2

Aftermath

~

LOGAN

Poor Kacie. The gossip flying around school today must be killing her. When she doesn't answer my texts, I decide to go search for her. It's not like there are many places she'd go to hide out. Only one comes to mind. It's where we all go during the school day to escape. The Orion Circle club room. After bounding up three flights of stairs, I pull out my key and open the door.

The moment I step into the doorway, I feel like I've been hit by a truck. I watch for a moment or two as my stomach plummets like a falling elevator. My chest hurts, and I can't seem to catch my breath. Without a sound, I back away and let the door close softly. *Click.*

It couldn't be, and yet I saw it with my own eyes. If anyone else told me, I would've accused them of lying.

Closing my eyes, I lean my forehead against the wall beside the door. The vision of them wrapped in a tight embrace is seared into my mind. Shaking my head as though it would erase the image, I try to find a rational explanation. But there isn't one. *Is there?* My best friend and my girlfriend were making out. Damn them. I can't believe I was worried about her, about how nervous she'd feel about kissing Daniel at rehearsal.

With a strangled groan I race down the stairs and out into the cool air. How long have they been doing this behind my back? My jaw clenches and my teeth gnash together. Damn, this hurts. Maybe I should go back and confront them…

I start to turn around, prepared to do just that but stop mid-motion. No, I have to cool off first. If I go in there now, they'll know how upset I am. Right now I'd like nothing better than to use Daniel's face as my own personal punching bag. Asshole deserves it. See how much the girls like him with two black eyes and a broken nose, maybe some missing teeth.

"Hey, Logan," a voice says behind me. "Are you heading to the cafeteria?"

Raven. Craptastic.

"No, I'm going to the gym to work out," I reply, looking over my shoulder.

Her frosty, blue eyes narrow into a glare. "You know, Kacie could use your support today."

"I think Kacie found all the support she needs elsewhere," I bite out before storming away.

Raven calls my name several times but doesn't chase after me. Thank God it wasn't Rebecca or we'd still be arguing. When I reach the locker room, I change into my workout clothes with a lot more banging than necessary. Hitting the lockers feels good. My foot connects with the lower locker. I can't find my blasted sparring gloves. With a groan I remember that I loaned them to Daniel. Figures. I grab the boxing tape and tape up my knuckles. I'd go without it, but if a coach catches me, I'd have my gym privileges suspended.

Stomping into the weight room, I almost let out a growl of frustration. Sam is at the heavy weight bag I need. None of the others are strong enough to handle my fury. I could try lifting, but I think I'm too restless to bother. Sam meets my gaze. His eyes widen, and he scurries away to the smaller teardrop bag. Hell, that's more his speed anyway.

The first punches I throw are hard but controlled. After a while, I settle into a rhythm of punches and kicks. The sounds around me melt away until all I hear is the slap of the bag against my hands and feet. It isn't until some sweat rolls into my eye that I come back to my senses. Wiping a hand across my forehead, I head to the locker room. After a quick shower, I dress and pull out my phone, steeling myself against the texts I know are there. Text after text telling me what a jerk I am for ditching Kacie. Not a single: *hey, Logan, are you okay?* The nastiest text is from Daniel. Hell I'd almost believe I didn't see what I know I saw based on his words.

Where the hell r u? Cici needs you. Ten minutes later: *U know things r crap, Get ur ass to lunch!* Five minutes later: *GFY.*

I collapse to the metal bench and open Kacie's texts.

R u ok? Followed by: *Where are u?* They continue about every minute or so, ten texts in all. Kacie hates texting. She must really be worried. My icy heart melts a bit, but then I remember how she looked in his arms, her lips locked with his. Damn her. How much can she possibly care when she can sneak around with him behind my back?

Only one voicemail, and it's from her.

"Logan, where are you? Is everything okay? I'm worried. Raven said you were really upset about something. Angry. Please call me."

I delete the message. Her voice was almost frantic. Let her stew. Maybe she'll figure it out on her own. The bell rings, but instead of heading to class, I decide to skip the rest of the day. I can't go to class and pretend everything is okay. Not when I feel like someone ripped my heart out and stomped it into dust. As I near my car, I curse under my breath.

Crows cover my Mustang. At least ten, maybe twenty. Why are Kacie's familiars hanging around me? I try to shoo them away, but they ignore my shout and waving arms. The largest, Kacie's special bird named Poe, sits on the roof of the car staring at me. Its unblinking gaze is unnerving. The bird watches me as I open the car door, putting my face within inches of its feathered body. I half expect it to attack, but it allows me to get into the car without incident.

Throwing the stick into reverse, I peel out of the parking space, my tires squealing on the pavement. The birds take flight, swirling around the car in a black mass before taking off into the sky. Slamming into first gear, I speed through the lot way too fast. The throaty roar of the engine is soothing, and for a brief moment I feel better. Then I'm forced to stop for a red light, and the bitterness returns full force. Turning on the radio, I switch the station to Octane and crank up the volume.

The drive home is nothing but a blur of movement and loud music. As I turn onto my street my heart lurches. Mom's Escalade is parked in the drive. She knows. Of course she knows. I've been broadcasting my emotions loud and clear. Mom's always had a knack for knowing when I need her—even across town. The front door opens, and she walks outside. Without a word, she comes to my side, placing her arm around my shoulders. I watch in silence as Kacie's crows land on my car, taking up their previous positions like I never left the school. *What does it mean?* They've never followed me around before.

"What happened, honey?" Mom asks in a soft voice. When I don't answer, she points to the birds. "Is there a reason that you know of for this display?"

"No."

One word. It's all I can get out through the lump in my throat. Being around Mom makes me want to fall into her arms and cry. I refuse to cry. Not over them. They don't deserve it.

"It's an omen," she murmurs as she leads me toward the front door. "They know something is going to happen to you. Your closeness to Kacie makes them almost your familiars as well."

"Kacie and I are through," I bite out, pushing the front door so hard it slams against the wall.

"The birds don't think so."

"Screw the birds!"

I throw my backpack to the floor and stomp into the kitchen. My stomach growls, though I don't really feel like eating. Mom walks in, the picture of calm beside my seething rage. Without a word she pulls out a can of tomato soup and lights the stove.

"Do you want a grilled cheese too?" she asks as though I didn't just scream at a flock of birds.

I open my mouth to say no, but instead mumble, "Yes, please."

She putters around the kitchen humming softly while I slump on a barstool at the counter. My head falls to my hands. I let it rest there while watching Mom, and listening to her soothing humming. It's an old Celtic tune, one she sang to me when I was little. Inch by inch, I feel my muscles unclench. The tension seeps from my body, and I feel empty. Drained. The aroma of tomato soup teases my nose, and my stomach twists in rebellion. I still don't think I can eat.

"Do you want to tell me what happened?" she asks, stirring the soup in the pot.

"No," I reply, letting my head fall to rest on the cool, granite countertop.

"You know talking about it will make you feel better," she says in a matter-of-fact tone.

"Will you leave me alone if I tell you?"

"Hmm, perhaps. I'll leave you alone right now if that's what you really want."

She places the grilled cheese on the counter before me. I don't want to eat. My stomach rumbles then roils. It seems it can't decide what it wants either. When she sets a mug of steaming tomato soup next to the plate, I take a deep breath, enjoying the way the steam tickles my nose. Shrugging, I take a sip of the hot soup. It's viscous yet tasty. I take another sip, pleased when my stomach remains quiet.

"I don't know where to start," I say before tearing off a bite of the grilled cheese. "It's been an unbelievably bad day."

"Start at the beginning."

"Kacie was a wreck this morning after drama. She found out she was going to be rehearsing a kissing scene with Daniel, and she freaked out."

"Yes, I can imagine that would be difficult for her. For being an actress, she's rather shy," Mom says, nodding.

"Well, things got worse," I say around a mouthful of sandwich. "By second period there was a betting pool about what would happen at rehearsal. I'm guessing lots of people will show up to watch."

"That's awful," Mom says, taking away my empty plate.

"Yeah, she was really upset," I murmur, remembering the frantic look on her face, and that was before I heard about the betting pool. Maybe she was so scared because she knew her secret was about to be revealed. "I heard from Rebecca that she walked out of her chemistry class, so I went looking for her. I didn't have to look far. I mean there's only one place she'd be."

"The Orion Circle room."

"Yeah. I opened the door and saw them." My eyes burn and I clench my hands into fists. "Kacie and Daniel. Together. Kissing."

She chuckles. "Oh, that must have been quite a shock."

"Why are you laughing?" I ask, turning my fury on her. "I walked in on my girlfriend and my best friend kissing, and you think it's funny?"

"Calm down, Logan," she says, stroking my arm. "You might be overreacting. I know it must have been devastating to see that. But think about it for a minute. Think about Kacie. She's been in our coven for two months, have you noticed anything about her behavior?"

"What the hell are you talking about?" I ask in an exasperated shout.

"Our Kacie likes to prepare, perhaps even over-prepare when it comes to anything public. I've never seen anyone practice a simple poem to the Goddess so many times."

I meet her gaze. She stares at me with a look of pity in her eyes, yet I can't help but think that it's me she's disappointed in.

"Just spit it out already," I order in a harsh tone, flinching when she gives me one of her death glares. "Please."

"Is it possible that Kacie was afraid about how she would react the first time she kissed Daniel on stage and wanted to practice?"

"That's absurd!" I shout, throwing my hands in the air. "It makes absolutely no sense. Why are you defending her? Do you realize how much she hurt me?"

"Yes, I do. And I'm not defending her," Mom says, her mouth set in a grim line. "I'm furious at her for doing this to you. For making you feel the way you do right now. But I think you leapt to an erroneous conclusion."

"So you really believe they were merely *rehearsing*," I say, making a quote motion with my fingers at the word rehearsing. "It didn't look like *rehearsing* to me. I was stunned for a moment. They never noticed me, too intent on each other. It was one hell of a long kiss for *rehearsing*."

"All I'm saying is that you need to talk to her," Mom says as she takes my empty mug away. She crosses over to the sink and rinses out the cup. When she turns back to look at me, her expression is soft. "Give them a chance to explain. They owe you that much. Daniel's been your best friend for years."

My phone rings before I have a chance to respond. Mr. Kincaid, the second-in-command of our Orion Circle chapter and our faculty advisor, according to caller ID.

"Hello, Mr. Kincaid."

"I see you skipped some classes this afternoon—including mine," Mr. Kincaid says. Crap. I forgot about physics. Of course Mr. Kincaid would know about my absence. "I covered for you with the office, but now I need you to do something."

"Of course, sir," I reply, glad I didn't receive the tongue lashing I expected.

"Anna can't make her three o'clock appointment this afternoon. I need you to go in her place." Anna, Mrs. Kincaid, our chapter's head, always vets the new clients. She rarely delegates the task.

"New client?" I ask, my pulse leaping a bit. I've never fielded a new client before even as an assistant. That the Kincaids trust me this much, it's an honor.

"Yes. I'll text you the address," he says, his voice muffled. I can hear some paper moving around. "A group of college girls at San Antonio University think they have a ghost problem. Go check it out and determine if we should set up an investigation. If we need to investigate, determine the appropriate response time."

"I'm on it," I reply, relieved to have something to do.

"Three o'clock," Mr. Kincaid says. "Don't be late. Oh, and Logan?"

"Yes?"

"Don't skip classes without permission. I won't cover for you again. I only did this time because Michelle was so insistent."

"Yes, sir," I say before hanging up.

Michelle is the empath in the Circle. Strong emotions overwhelm her. I thought I steered clear of her, but obviously not clear enough. While I felt like a bowling ball was crushing my heart, she probably felt it too. Craptastic.

3

Rehearsal

～

KACIE

The auditorium is filled to almost overflowing. Mr. Holmes encourages the student body to watch our rehearsals, so there's little I can do about it. I feel like I'm under a microscope. Everything I say, every move I make is under scrutiny. It's beginning to drive me mad.

It would have been much better had we started with the kissing scene, but no, Mr. Holmes is doing everything in order. I run through the song and dance number on autopilot. I've practiced it so many times in my bedroom, it's second nature now. At least I look good for this part of rehearsal.

After the song ends, I step back to wait for the director to call the next scene. My mind wanders, returning to dwell on Logan. He missed lunch and hasn't answered his phone. Raven ran into him on the way to lunch. She acted so guarded about him. All she said was that he was upset about something, and she didn't know what. I can't help but worry. His car wasn't in the parking lot after lunch and neither were my birds. *Where could he have gone?*

The moment I've been dreading for days arrives with much fanfare, drawing me out of my thoughts.

"Okay, let's check out the chemistry between my two stars," Mr. Holmes says, clapping his hands together. "Start about two lines away from the kiss."

Hoots and hollers flood the auditorium as the audience shows their approval that the moment of truth has finally arrived. Really, don't they have anything better to do than torment me? I'm so relieved that Daniel and I practiced earlier. Otherwise, I think I might've run from the stage. He meets my gaze and gives me a wink as we walk toward each other to center stage. I barely register him saying his line. Mine comes out in a clear voice, giving me an internal confidence boost. It's time.

I close the distance between us, placing one hand on his chest and the other at his nape. We gaze into each other's eyes for a moment before I wrap my arm around his neck and push up onto my toes. The moment I press my lips to his, he responds by wrapping both arms around me. The kiss is chaste, but I doubt it appears that way to the audience. I count slowly to five in my head like we agreed then pull away.

"Brilliant!" Mr. Holmes shouts. "Absolutely brilliant. I'm so pleased—I'm dismissing everyone early today. Happy Friday."

"I think Mr. Holmes has a hot date," Daniel whispers in my ear.

My reply is drowned out by the roar of the crowd all talking over one another. A wry half-smile forms on my lips as I watch the arguments breaking out all over the place. These asshats deserve whatever they get. I heard the odds were two to one that I'd run off the stage. I'm glad we screwed up their idiotic betting pool.

"Logan isn't here," I murmur, glancing around the theater.

"Were you expecting him?" Daniel asks over the noisy crowd.

"Yeah, we were supposed to go out for dinner tonight," I reply, biting my lip. My phone vibrates in the pocket of my blue jeans. I pull it out, frowning when I see Rebecca's name. "Hey, what's up?"

"Logan's on assignment and needs our help asap," she blurts out in an excited voice.

"Is he okay?" Worry jars my heart into a rapid beat.

"Yeah, I think so," she says. "Look, I'll text you the address. You're with Daniel, right?" She pauses for a couple beats. "How did *it* go?"

"Great," I reply with a snicker while watching the rowdy crowd exit the auditorium.

"Well that's a relief, anyway. Ask Daniel if he can drive you to the SAU campus. We could definitely use his help with the spirit board."

Spirit board? This could be very bad. "Are you free tonight?" I glance up at Daniel, and he nods. "Yeah, text me the address. We're on our way now."

"Hurry," she says before disconnecting.

"What's going on?" Daniel asks as we head backstage to get out backpacks.

"Logan is on assignment and asked for backup." My voice shakes, betraying my nerves. "I'm worried about him."

"Yeah, me too," he says, grabbing his bag, "I have a bad feeling about this. I think I know why Logan was angry earlier and why he bailed."

"Are you going to share?" I ask when he remains silent.

"No, not yet." We walk out the backstage door into the parking lot. Daniel's SUV is right in front surrounded by his bimbo groupies. "Ah, hell."

They flutter around him, cooing and whining. It's enough to make me vomit.

"Sorry, ladies, as you can see I'm busy." Daniel shoulders past them. They don't take the hint, and he can barely open the door wide enough to shove his backpack through.

"God, don't you tramps have anything better to do than bug my guy?" Raven asks, arriving on the scene with a nasty scowl on her face. She yanks the car door, opening it wider, hitting a couple of the gathered groupies. "You know, like sacrificing babies or puppies or something."

"He's not your guy," the leader says, sneering, "are you, Daniel?" She tosses her blond hair with a red, manicured hand.

"No comment," Daniel says as he squeezes into the front seat. "And for the record, you girls really need to find someone else to stalk. It's getting old."

"It got old long ago," Raven snaps. She hops into the backseat and slams the door, hard.

I almost feel bad for the four girls, watching their faces fall. But really, Daniel should have said something to them before now. After getting into the passenger seat and closing the door, I toss my backpack into the backseat next to Raven. We travel in silence for a while since Daniel doesn't turn on the stereo. I'm not used to being in a car without any music.

"For the record, I've asked them to leave me alone before," Daniel says with an exasperated groan. "It's like the challenge makes them more rabid or some-thing. Lately I've just been trying to ignore them."

"Sorry, Daniel. I don't blame you," Raven says, lean-ing forward. "Living next to the president of your fan club got old real quick."

"Hey, at least you don't have to worry about me ever dropping by."

"Oh no, that's the least of my worries." Raven flops against the backseat. "Queen Bitch had the gall to drop by last weekend with a Daniel questionnaire. Like I'd give her any information about you."

"You're kidding." Daniel sounds dumbfounded.

"Yeah, I wish. But no, she really did and there were twenty-five Daniel-related questions."

While they continue their conversation about Daniel's annoying groupies, I text Logan.

Hey, u ok?

I wait for a long thirty seconds then my phone buzzes a reply.

No.

Just no. Nothing else. No explanation, no details, just no.

Care to share?

This time the reply comes faster.

No.

Tears burn my eyes. Logan has never been so dismissive before. Something is most definitely wrong... but what?

4

Sorority Sisters

LOGAN

When I pull up to the house, I have to double check the address Mr. Kincaid texted me. The Greek letters *Rho Gamma Pi* are emblazoned on the front of the house in bold, blue lettering. He sent me to a sorority house. A dark voice in the back of my mind whispers that this is the perfect opportunity to get even with Kacie. Shaking my head, I silence it. That is not who I am, nor who I want to be.

Crows settle down on the eaves, in the oak trees, and on the porch railing. It seems Kacie's familiars don't plan to leave me to face whatever lurks in that house alone.

The moment I'm out of the Mustang, two attractive, brunette co-eds race from the house, making a beeline for my car. They look enough alike to be real sisters. Both have light brown hair, one falling to her waist in waves, the other as short as mine. Their doe-brown eyes are wide, haunted. I manage to hide my shock when they both fall against my body and wrap their arms around me. Not that I'd normally complain about two pretty girls hugging me, but I'm here on Circle business. This is starting to look like some sort of sorority stunt rather than a real case.

That all changes when I realize one of them is crying.

"I'm Logan Finley with the Orion Circle," I say while trying to decide what to do with my hands. When I give in and wrap my arms around them, the other girl starts sobbing too. "I can't help you if you don't tell me what's wrong."

"I th-th-thought…" The girl with short hair pulls away and gazes at me with teary eyes. "I thought it was a toy," she blurts out before burying her face back against my shoulder.

"What was a toy?" I ask, patting her back.

"The b-b-board," the other girl says.

Tension spreads through my shoulders and up my neck. There's really only one type of board that would cause a problem that I'd need to investigate. Any sympathy I had for these girls is quickly fading. I hate stupid. Only an idiot messes with something they have no clue about.

"Let's go inside and talk," I say, biting my lip to keep from saying what I really want to say.

"No!" they both shout together. The crows ruffle their feathers and flap their wings, but remain silent.

"No?" I ask, glancing around. We're going to attract attention at this rate. Lots of black birds, sobbing sorority girls… it's like a bad horror movie.

"*They're* in there," the short-haired girl says.

"How about we sit on the grass then," I suggest, hoping to get this situation under control.

Perhaps I'm a bit out of my league here. I sag a bit in relief when they both nod their agreement. For some reason, I expected the girls to let go of me so we could walk over to the small patch of grass in the front yard. No such luck. They continue clinging to me as I inch forward. Whenever I dreamed of having two girls hanging all over me, it was never like this. It usually involved a party and laughter, not ghosts and tears. We reach the patch of green, and I ease them both to the ground, thankful when they release their firm hold on my shirt.

"Okay, let's start with your names," I say, hoping to bring them out of their panic with an easy question.

"Kendra," says the girl with short hair.

"Melissa."

"Great. I'm Logan. I'm here to help you." I channel everything I remember about my mother and her easygoing interrogation techniques. "Tell me what happened."

"It was just a toy," Kendra says through a sob. "I mean I got it at a toy store at the outlet mall."

"It wasn't supposed to work," Melissa adds, putting her arm around Kendra.

"A spirit board," I bite out through a clenched jaw.

I really hate those things. Dangerous supernatural objects should never be packaged for children. It's a full on crime. I don't give a flying rat's ass whether you believe in the paranormal or not. What CEO says, *Kids should try channeling spirits. Let's put out a spirit board and stick it in with the board games.* Utter crap on so many levels, I can't begin to count.

Kendra nods. "Yeah."

"How could we know it would work?" Melissa says with an angry glare. Good I can handle angry better than sobbing.

"It said 'glow in the dark' on the box." Kendra wrings her hands together. "I mean, that's like a toy, right?"

"This isn't your fault," I say, and actually mean it. "Nothing that dangerous should ever be marketed to children. You couldn't know the consequences."

Kendra glances over her shoulder. "There's something bad in the house now."

"Real bad," Melissa agrees.

As if to justify her statement, a loud crash sounds from within the sorority house. Several girls run out screaming. They collapse on the grass beside Melissa and Kendra, a tangle of limbs and hysterical crying. Crows take to the sky, circling the house and *cawing* their displeasure. I gnaw on my cheek to keep from screaming and pull out my phone to call for backup.

"We really need to go inside so I can check out the spirit board," I say in as calm a voice as I can muster. It's hard to concentrate with five cute girls falling all over me.

"I'll take you to the board," Kendra says, straightening her back. "Come on, Melissa. I'm not going alone."

"Will you keep me safe?" Melissa asks in a hoarse whisper. She gazes at me with wide eyes while caressing my leg through my jeans.

"I have a girlfriend," I blurt out without thinking.

Yeah, one who kisses your best friend.

"Oh, too bad," Melissa says, though she continues drawing small shapes on my leg.

"Right, well, we need to go check out the spirit board before my backup arrives." I push her hand away. Rising to my feet, I walk toward the open front door. "Are you coming?"

"Um, no, I don't think so." Melissa lets out a shaky laugh. "I've had enough psycho girl spirits for one day."

I somehow resist the urge to smack my forehead with my palm. "You know who the spirits are?"

"Well, yeah," Melissa says, inching closer to me. She snuggles against my side, wrapping her arm around my back. "They told us their names, and that they were murdered."

"First of all, back off," I tell Melissa in a gruff voice.

"Do I distract you?" She gives me a coy smile.

"Yes, but not in the way you seem to want to." I bite my lip to keep from snapping. My words have the desired effect even with my calm tone. Melissa backs away as though I drenched her in ice water. "I have to go get the spirit board. We'll need to bind it in order to calm the spirits enough to talk to them."

"Yeah, they don't want to talk, just throw things around," Kendra says, shaking her head. As though to emphasize her words, another loud crash reverberates from within the house.

"Where is the board?" I ask, somehow managing to keep my features blank and my voice neutral.

"In the kitchen at the back of the house," Kendra replies, pointing her finger toward the door. "In the sink. We tried to burn it."

Well, at least now I know part of why the spirits are so pissed off. My teeth gnash together in an effort to keep any lectures at bay. Now isn't a good time, and I doubt these girls will ever play with a spirit board again anyway.

"Stay here," I order before heading toward the door.

The moment my foot crosses the threshold, the door slams shut, smashing my foot and knocking me backward. As I stare up at the bright red door, it opens again, revealing a wispy, silver image of a girl with long hair. Her back is to me. When she turns around, I swallow hard, hiding my shock behind a blank mask. She appears in her death state, which given her power level, is a choice. If she thinks to shock me, she'll have to try harder than this. The right side of her head is caved in, and her nose isn't in the center of her face anymore. Bones stick out through her arms and legs. Her dress is in tatters. Perhaps my cold scrutiny makes her uneasy. She disappears leaving behind an icy breeze.

I glance over my shoulder at the cowering girls. Though they still appear afraid, I'm guessing based on the lack of hysterical shrieking that they didn't see the ghost. Steeling my nerve, I push my body across the threshold. The air is so thick; it's like moving through water. The moment my body is inside the house, the door slams shut again. Probably for the best—now I don't have to deal with the sorority sisters. A scream echoes down the staircase followed by thumping footsteps.

Two girls race down the hardwood stairs practically falling over each other in their attempt to flee whatever chases them. I expect them to run to the door, but instead both plaster themselves to my sides. I'm beginning to feel like I'm in some thirteen-year-old's wet dream. Nothing appears behind them on the staircase, and I let out an exasperated sigh that sounds like a growl. The girls both shriek and clutch at me when the front door bangs open by itself. A blunt invitation to leave.

I lead the now quiet girls to the door and usher them outside. The moment we cross the threshold, the door slams shut hard enough to rattle the frame. After pushing the rescued girls toward their friends, I try to open it. Two sore fists and a stubbed toe later, I acknowledge the fact that the spirits have no intention of letting me back inside. Seems the only reason I was allowed inside to begin with was to assist in pest removal.

I make my way to a giant oak tree at the edge of the yard, as far away from the annoying sorority girls as I can get. Crows land in the tree as I sink to the soft dirt amid the roots. I want to yell at them to make them scatter. They're a bitter reminder of Kacie and her betrayal. Instead I lean my head against the rough bark, grinding my teeth together when several girls approach my sanctuary.

Before I can say a word, Poe lands on the ground nearby, cawing and flapping his wings at the frightened co-eds. They scuttle backward, returning to the tight-knit circle near the driveway. Despite my sadness and anger, a smile creeps across my face when Poe perches on my leg. The large crow watches me while making a soft cooing noise. I run my fingers down his soft back, not caring how odd I must look petting a crow. Nothing to do now but wait for backup.

5

Chaos

~

KACIE

We arrive at our destination amid utter chaos. Sorority girls cover the front yard of the house—some pacing, some crying, lots of shouting and cursing. There must be at least twenty of them out here. A small crowd has gathered on the sidewalk, watching the odd behavior. So much for keeping a low profile. If we don't get these girls under control, we'll all end up on the evening news.

My silver bracelet pulses like a second heartbeat—fast, steady bursts of power. There's lots of negative energy here. Between the frightened girls and whatever scared them, it sent my bracelet into overtime. I caress the silver with my fingertips, hoping to calm the rapid rhythm. This ancient relic had been passed down a long line of witches before it chose me two months ago. While it does warn of impeding spiritual danger, it also becomes impossible to remove in the presence of any perceived threat. At times it seems more like a shackle than a bracelet.

When I try to remove it, the clasp won't budge—it has become a shackle once again. Not a good sign at all. The last time this happened, I was up against the Foxblood Demon and almost died. My coven high priestess, Mrs. Finley, says the bracelet is a gift from the Goddess. Some gift. I resist the urge to scratch at my wrist where the silver shimmies and vibrates.

My thoughts immediately fly to Logan, and I survey the scene. Hours of built-up tension melts away when I spy him sitting under an oak tree near the property line safe and sound. He leans against the trunk, watching the girls through half-closed eyes. My familiars are perched in the tree branches, keeping a silent vigil over him. Their mere presence makes my pulse race fast enough to rival the bracelet's quick pace. Something is wrong, or they wouldn't be here with him.

As soon as Daniel puts the SUV in park, I leap out and race to Logan's side. I've been worried about him for hours. It's not until I'm towering over him that I realize I'm torn between hugging him and screaming at him for making me worry.

"Logan, you... I..." I trail off at his dark glare.

"I was there," he murmurs, his golden-brown eyes never leaving mine. "I saw you with him."

"What are you—" Halfway through my question it hits me. "You saw me kissing Daniel in the club room?"

"Yes."

"Oh God, Logan. I'm so sorry. I should have told you." The words tumble from my mouth in rapid succession. "It was kind of a last minute decision."

"What?" He looks at me with such loathing mixed with sorrow.

"I was a nervous wreck," I murmur, sinking to the ground beside him. "The bets were making me fall apart. I love acting, but rehearsals are hard for me. I perform best when the stage lights are on. With the house lights on and a hundred pairs of eyes staring at me… well sometimes it's really hard."

"You were rehearsing." His lips are in a firm line, his brow creased. He doesn't believe me.

"Please believe me, Logan." I place my hand on his arm, caressing him through his thermal shirt. "Daniel and I would *never* hurt you like that."

"I *was* hurt. God, it hurt," he says in a choked whisper. "I felt like my chest was being crushed."

"I'm so sorry, Logan." I wrap my arms around his neck. My heart falls a bit when he doesn't return my embrace. "I swear to you. The only thing I noticed while kissing him was the placement of my hands and the counting in my head."

"Counting?"

"Yeah. Daniel told me to count to a slow five in my head before releasing the kiss," I admit, leaning my forehead against his cheek.

"You were counting in your head." Logan makes a noise that sounds suspiciously like a laugh. "You kiss the amazing Daniel Westin, and all you think about is how long until you can stop?"

"Um, yeah." I pull back to look at him. My eyes widen at the adorable smirk gracing his face. "If the kiss was too short, Mr. Holmes would've made us do it over and over until we got it right. Then I'm sure one of the bet options would have happened. I wanted it to be perfect to begin with. Then I could walk away with the last laugh."

"What do you think about when I kiss you?"

A warm flush shoots up my neck. "I, uh… you, nothing. I can't really think too much when you kiss me." The blush spreads from my neck across my cheeks. "When it's over I sometimes worry about whether my legs will support me."

"You are so beautiful when you blush," he murmurs, brushing a light kiss over my lips.

"I'm sorry I hurt you."

"Don't apologize anymore." He kisses my forehead. "Had I gone with instinct and followed through with option number three, this entire event would have wrapped up much quicker."

"You heard about the betting pool." The flush on my cheeks deepens from anger. "Asshats, the whole lot of them. Those vultures all showed up for the rehearsal. You should have seen their faces when Daniel and I nailed the kiss on the first try with absolutely no embarrassing issues."

I pause for a moment, trying to remember what option number three was. When it hits me, I pull away and stare into Logan's eyes.

"Option three was you beating up Daniel. You wanted to do that?"

"It was my first instinctive reaction," he replies, unable to mask the sorrow in his eyes. "I went to the gym and beat on a weight bag for a while instead. Then went home only to be stalked by your damnable crows. They were all over my car at school and followed me home, then all the way here. How the hell did they know I might be in danger with this case?"

"I don't think they were with you because of the danger." I glance up at my feathered friends. "I think they were reacting to your mood. They were worried about you."

"They're crows."

"You know better than that," I murmur before kissing his cheek. "You're the one who taught me that familiars are more than mere animals. There's something supernatural about their behavior. They were with you because they were concerned."

"I wish I had a familiar," he says, glancing up at the crows covering the branches over his head.

"Until you get your own, it appears I'm sharing."

Daniel walks over, eyeing us with a wary look. "We okay, Logan?"

"Yeah," Logan says, rising to his feet. He holds his hand down to me, and pulls me up, snaking an arm around my back.

"I would never…" Daniel says, trailing off.

"I know."

"So…" Daniel shoves his hands into the pockets of his jeans while he rocks back and forth.

"This might be bad," Logan says, pointing at the house. "Three furious spirits are tearing this place apart."

Before I can ask any questions, Carl and Rebecca arrive in the Circle van with the ghost hunting equipment. Something tells me we don't need the cameras and EMF detector for this one. Though, maybe Carl will finally get his proof on camera. Logan takes my hand, entwining our fingers while our auras and powers mingle together. We gain strength from one another, and it seems to work much better when we're touching. Raven stalks over, her expression stormy. Looks like our sorority clients annoyed her.

"Okay, so after Logan's failed attempt at nabbing the spirit board, I'm guessing our ghosts don't like guys much. I'm heading into the house to grab the board. Hopefully they let me in," Raven says, her lips in a firm line. "It's in the kitchen. Those idiots over there tried to burn it in the sink when the ghosts popped out. Good thing they didn't succeed."

Destroying a spirit board is never a good idea, not unless you're looking to trap the spirit you summon to this plane. We need to banish the spirit, and then destroy the board. It will be burned to ash, the ashes scattered in several different places, at least one running water.

"I'll be waiting," Daniel says. Though he tries to appear nonchalant, his face pales.

Poor guy is going to have to touch the board to get a reading. I don't envy his clairsentient power one bit. When I glance at Logan, he gives a little nod. I take Daniel's hand in mine, lending him our combined strength. Anything powerful enough to make this much racket is not weak. Spirits are intangible—it can take years for a ghost to learn to manipulate the environment.

"If I'm not out in five minutes..." Raven trails off, leaving the worst case scenario unsaid.

"We'll come in after you," Daniel says, giving her a little salute.

She straightens her back and walks toward the wide-open front door. With one last glance over her shoulder, she crosses the threshold. My breath catches in my throat when a blue armchair flies out through the front bay window. Logan's fingers tighten around mine. Daniel races to the chair, placing his palm on the arm. A small tremor twitches along his jawline when he glances back at us. It looks like we're in for a rough night.

6
Three Nasty Ghosts

~

LOGAN

Tension rises as everyone stops to stare at the armchair now lying in the front yard. Though the sorority girls are frightened, their overall fear level doesn't increase much. Mine soars along with my hammering heart. Only a powerful entity could throw a chair out the window, but it's probably best to keep that little tidbit to myself. No point in scaring the sorority more. Kacie's fingers clench my hand to the point of pain, but I don't care, nor do I let go. We will need to combine our power to deal with whatever currently occupies the *Rho Gamma Pi* house.

I look on in horror as Daniel collapses against the armchair. Carl and Rebecca drag him away, but it's impossible to miss the haunted look in his eyes. Every peek into the unknown carries a risk—we all know and accept that. It doesn't make times like this any easier though. Kacie releases my hand and kneels down on the grass beside Daniel. When she pulls him into a hug, a surge of jealousy rushes through me. *Unwarranted*, I remind myself and potentially hazardous. We are a team and need to support each other, and yet all I can think of at the moment is wrenching her away from him.

"I'm going to check on Raven," I murmur to Kacie, taking off before I can hear her reply.

My gaze travels to the sorority sisters, all huddled together near the driveway. Twenty-three of them, yet I couldn't get a coherent answer about what happened. Melissa and Kendra mumbled something about murder but refused to elaborate.

"Rebecca!" I yell over the banging from the house and the sobs of the girls.

"Need help?" she asks with a wary glance at the house.

"I need you and Carl to find out as much as you can about a murder that may have occurred at *Rho Gamma Pi*—" I cringe when a small end table hits the door-jamb. "It's all I could get out of them. Try talking to them. You seem to have a way with difficult interrogations."

"My specialty," she replies, flashing a wicked grin.

Her smile is scary, definitely more so than many ghosts I've faced. Rebecca has a take-no-prisoners attitude coupled with fierce intelligence. I know she thinks she has no paranormal powers, but I think she's a human lie detector.

"Huge EMF spike!" Carl shouts, waving the EMF detector in the air.

That's it. I can't wait for Raven any longer. Mr. Kincaid's voice echoes in my mind, calling me stupid for rushing in not knowing what's in there. But I'm in charge of this fiasco… I never should've let her run in without more information. Steeling my shoulders, I cross the threshold into the house.

I stop and survey the scene in seconds, taking in the ridiculous amount of damage. The living room is trashed: sofa overturned, lamps broken on the floor, and the front window shattered by the flying armchair. No sign of Raven, but the girls said they were using the board in the kitchen. As I walk down the hall toward the back of the house, a ceramic figurine flies at me. I duck just in time, and it grazes the top of my hair. I'm finding it difficult to believe spirits summoned from a spirit board by amateurs could be this powerful.

The family room is in a similar state to the living room. When I spy the sixty-inch TV on the floor in a smashed mess my heart thumps faster. These are powerful spirits or maybe even a rogue gang. That TV had to weigh over one hundred pounds, and it's a good twelve feet from the entertainment center. No sign of Raven in here either.

A fierce wind blows from the kitchen, slamming me against the wall. So much power. None of this makes any sense!

"Raven." I try to call out, but my voice comes out a hoarse croak.

My body is freed as the wind dies down, and I race toward the kitchen. Something shoves me from behind, sending me reeling across the tile floor. I manage to rotate myself at the last second so my shoulder impacts the wall instead of my head. The wind stops the moment I hit the wall. As I rub my sore shoulder, a loud scream pierces the silence. My stomach drops at the sheer terror in that scream. Raven.

Leaping to my feet, I search the large kitchen for her. When my eyes land on her, I blink a few too many times. This shouldn't be possible.

"Hang on, Raven," I call out to her form suspended in midair near the ceiling.

"Hang on? Really?" Her arms are splayed out to the sides, her long, black hair floating around her like a mermaid underwater. Though she tries to project confidence with her words, I can tell from her face that she's terrified.

"Release her at once!" I yell at the invisible spirits. "She has done nothing to you."

"Don't you think I already tried that?" Raven bites out in between gasping breaths.

"St. Michael, the archangel, def—" I start the prayer, but something crashes into me, knocking the wind from my lungs as I'm slammed into the floor. It takes a few dazed seconds to realize it's Raven's body crushing me. "Can you move?"

"I don't know." She rolls off me despite her words, groaning. "Those damned spirits. Madder than cornered rattlesnakes."

"I can't feel anything but intense hatred and fury." I push to my feet, ignoring the searing pain in my side. After hauling Raven up by the arm, I drag her toward the back door.

"Wait!" she yells, yanking her arm away. "The board." Raven disappears beneath the long oak table. A few seconds later, she pops out holding the spirit board.

"Come on," I shout when I feel the spirits returning for round two. "Crap, too late." An invisible force plows into me, pushing me back into the unforgiving wall. "Raven, run!"

Something hits me in the ribs, banging my body into the wall once, twice, three times. My head spins from the impact. At least Raven made it out. A white mist fills my vision, and I blink several times. It doesn't go away, only becomes sharper, more focused. Her form is wispy, ethereal. She would be beautiful were her lips not turned into a vicious sneer. I lie on the ground, waiting for her to make her move while she floats around me.

"She lied," the ghost whispers in a grating voice so at odds with her glowing visage.

"Who lied?" I swallow around the lump of dread in my throat.

My instincts scream at me to run, but I'm trapped on this hard, tile floor until my head stops spinning. I take a deep breath and bite back a yelp. My fingers fly to my left side. A hiss escapes my lips from the sharp pain—my ribs are broken or bruised. Either way it hurts like hell.

"Earlier outside, your girlfriend, she lied," the ghost girl informs me, her face contorted in malicious glee. "I can't believe you fell for it! Kissing that hunk was a rehearsal? Damn you'd have to be a total chump to fall for that."

I ignore her mocking words. I trust Kacie and Daniel. *Right?* With a loud groan, I push myself to my feet, clutching my side. Turning my back on the now cackling specter, I limp from the kitchen.

"Aww, did I hurt your little feelings?" she asks in a mocking tone as she appears in front of me.

My breath flies out through gritted teeth. After all these years, I should be past gasping in surprise whenever a ghost pops in, but I guess it's just one of those things that will always bug me. Right now, this girl seems to be a bit more than I can handle. Dirty trick, playing on my insecurity. She must be worried about what we might do to evict her.

"Sometimes the truth hurts," another female voice says from behind me as I'm shoved forward.

This time I'm unable to hold back a startled cry as pain sears through my side. I whip around to confront the newest presence. She floats above the ground, a mocking smile on her mangled face. The entire left side of her head is caved in, and her limbs bend at impossible angles. Another ghost appears beside her, pristine and white with long, flowing hair. She looks like she should be running through a meadow, maybe picking flowers, rather than glaring down at me with a scowl marring her face. Four dark scratches cover each cheek from her eyes down to her mouth. They almost appear self-inflicted, like whatever happened to her was so awful that she scratched her own cheeks with her fingernails.

"Did we break him?" the new spirit asks, moving within inches of my face. A frigid breeze accompanies her hand as she waves it in my face. "Darn, and he was so cute too."

My mind reels in confusion. Never, in all my investigations, have I come across such an odd trio of spirits. Not only are they able to manipulate the physical world, but they speak so clearly. I can't begin to imagine the amount of power they'd need to command to perform such a feat.

Silence seems to work, and I allow the three ghosts to think I've lost my mind, while I try to make sense of what I'm seeing. They whisper to each other, pointing my way every few words. I've heard of spirit boards opening portals to all sorts of weirdness... but this?

7

Rescue

~

KACIE

Raven bursts from the house, the spirit board cradled
to her chest. She lurches across the front yard, and I
concentrate on the front door, waiting for Logan to
appear. As the seconds tick by my throat closes, making
it difficult to breathe. He's trapped in the house with
those evil *things*.

"Logan!" I cry out, rushing to the open door. The
door slams shut in my face. "No!"

I pound on the wood until my fists ache. This isn't
accomplishing anything. I need to get inside now. While
I don't know exactly what's going on here, my bracelet
is pulsing enough to jar my arm. I can't leave Logan
alone in there.

"Cici, stop," Daniel says, grabbing my hands before
I can attack the door again.

"Let me go, Daniel! Logan needs me."

"Yes, he does, but you need to calm down if you want to help him." He rubs the side of my hands where the skin is raw. "It's bad, weird, and I don't know what. These spirits are affecting you. Look at your hands."

My head begins to clear, like a fog lifting. "What happened?" I ask, shaking my head. "I feel… strange."

"These ghosts aren't, uh, normal," Daniel says as he pulls me away from the porch.

"There's such a thing as normal ghosts?" Raven asks. Though she tries to scoff and act tough, her face is ashen.

Daniel helps me sit down on the grass. "You need to focus, Cici."

"My head feels so hazy." I run my fingers through the cool blades of grass. The feel of the grass helps ground me in the present, and the odd haze surrounding me finally fades away. Deep breaths calm my racing heart. Now that my head is clear, I realize my utter folly. I was banging on a locked door when there was a massive broken window six feet away.

"Better?" Daniel runs his hand over my forehead like he expects a fever. "Your skin is much cooler now. You sure worked yourself into a frenzy."

"I had help," I mumble, staring at the ground to avoid his eyes. Those miscreant spirits will pay. "Those are not your average, everyday ghosts in there. Have you touched the spirit board?"

"No. I won't be doing it here." Daniel runs a hand through his disheveled black hair. "I'm afraid they might gain control over me if I do."

"We need to regroup away from here," Rebecca says, towering over us with her hands on her hips. "We've drawn a crowd. We're gonna be on the news tonight if we don't quiet this mess down. Suggestions?"

"Security guard?" Carl asks as he drags the armchair away from the broken window.

"Not good enough," Rebecca says, glancing around. "We have to get rid of the sorority sisters and all these morons milling around."

"Termite tent." Raven waves her hand at the house. "My grandma had her house tented last year, and the threat of poison was enough to keep everyone away."

"Like in that X-Files with the monster guy who covers the house with that red and white tent, then has his way with the female occupants?" Carl asks, his voice shaking in excitement.

"Um, yes, and eww." Raven pulls her phone from her jacket pocket. "I'll call Mr. Kincaid and get it set up."

I watch her storm off toward the street. "Inside. Now. I'm not leaving Logan with those ghosts one second longer."

Daniel drapes his leather jacket over the broken bay window. "Then may I suggest you climb in through here rather than banging more on the door?"

He boosts me up, and I half-stumble, half-jump through. Something knocks me forward as I land, sending my body careening into a nearby, upended sofa. My elbow cracks against the wooden leg, and pain shoots up into my shoulder. I bite my lip to keep from yelling. Those ghosts won't get a reaction from me... well not much of one anyway.

"Stay out there," I yell to Daniel who is clamoring through the opening. "They aren't playing nice."

He gives me a quizzical look before easing his body back through the window. "I'll wait here. Hurry, Cici." His calm words belie the raw concern radiating from his eyes.

After a few deep breaths, I push to my feet and head toward the back of the house looking for Logan. My head spins, and my vision blurs. The air is so heavy around me, like a tangible pressure. When I reach the family room, I can't contain my gasp. Utter destruction. I'm about to continue to the kitchen when I hear a muffled groan.

"Logan, is that you?" I call out into the eerie silence.

"Over here." His reply is soft, pained.

Furniture is stacked haphazardly in an amazing array, like a real-life Jenga game, ready to tumble with even the slightest touch. I squeeze between an end table and the remains of a big-screen TV, careful to keep my body from touching them. Pieces of glass from several broken lamps crunch under my feet as I follow the sound of Logan's labored breathing. I find him sprawled against the fireplace, the brick mantel in pieces covering his body.

"Oh God, Logan, where are you hurt?" I ask while flinging bricks from his body.

"My ribs... bruised or broken... my fingers..." He holds up his left hand. His middle and ring fingers both appear to be broken. His eyes widen. "Crap! They're back."

My hair whips around my face as the spirits appear in a small whirlwind. Dark whispers fill the air around us, too soft to make out the words but menacing nonetheless. Ignoring them, I continue to remove the bricks from Logan's battered body. Fear fills his eyes, and I silently implore him to ignore the intruders. They've had enough attention for one day. There's a good chance our fear is feeding them, fueling their power. Once the smaller bricks are removed, I see the large piece of mantel keeping Logan pinned to the ground.

"I think if we push this together, we can roll it off your legs." Before I can get my weight behind the mantel and push, one of the spirits plows into me, knocking me on my back. Something inside me snaps. Anger, humiliation, fear, sorrow—all the emotions I've felt during this annoying day at school and here with the uncooperative spirits—it all swirls around until it explodes. "Back off!" I scream at the invisible phantoms lurking nearby. "Leave us alone!" My aura flares around my body, an angry red. Within moments the air stops moving, and the oppressive weight lifts.

"They're gone," Logan says, relief flooding his eyes. He helps me push the mantel off of his legs, and lurches to unsteady feet. "I hit my head a few times while those bitches were flinging me around."

I brush brick dust from his forehead, careful to avoid the deep scrape on his temple. The blood has dried in streaks down his left cheek and neck. Though I want to check him over, assess his injuries, we need to get out of here before the ghosts return.

"How many fingers am I holding up?" I ask, holding up my index finger.

"Eleven," he replies chuckling. The snicker is followed by a cough which causes a pained groan.

I wrap his arm over my shoulders, supporting some of his weight. "Let's get out of here."

8

Research

∽

LOGAN

Two bruised ribs, two busted fingers, and a knee swollen up the size of a cantaloupe. And of course I can't forget the lovely gash on my left temple and the black eye. At least I didn't need stitches. I lie in the dark, trying to resist the urge to toss and turn. Whenever I move, a sharp pain shoots through my side. Maybe I should just take the pain pills Dr. Hayes gave me. No, there's no way I'm staying out of this hunt, not after what those vicious phantoms did to me. Pills will only cloud my mind.

Mom and Dad are down the hall arguing... probably over my safety. I can't tell; the thick walls muffle their words. Ever since my sister, Clarissa, died my parents have become a tad overprotective. Perhaps my injuries today were too much for them to deal with.

Clarissa... it's been almost five years, yet it seems like yesterday. Images fill my mind—violence, blood, screams. I shut down the thought, slamming the memories away deep down. I can't deal with the sorrow and regret now.

My cell buzzes. *You didn't take your meds did you.*

Kacie. She seems to know me pretty well. *No.*

See the news?

Hard to miss.

The Circle sure can spin a story.

Had to do something to explain a bunch of screaming sorority girls. My head still aches from the incessant screeching.

Yeah, but crickets and cockroaches?? Eww!

I can almost feel her shiver. Poor Kacie finds insects much scarier than ghosts. *Explains the extermination tent.*

Greek prank gone wrong—story at 10.

If only they knew the truth—now that would be a newsflash—ghosts gone wild.

Lol, try to sleep. Meeting at 9. Know u won't wanna miss it.

My lips curl into a smile. Well, at least my girlfriend isn't coddling me, acting like I'm useless because I'm injured. *Pick u up at 8:30.*

Several moments later. *Daniel will pick us both up. Driving might be hard.*

She's right. Craptastic. Now I can't even drive my own car. And Daniel. I shouldn't be mad at him, I know I shouldn't… but I keep seeing him kissing Kacie. Damn it, why can't I get that awful picture out of my head? I guess I wait too long to reply.

Logan you ok?

I lie. *Fine. Get some sleep.*

You too. Night ♥

Night ♥

I toss the phone aside. Silence fills the house now. It looks like my parents gave up on their argument and went to sleep. Stifling a groan, I push myself up into a sitting position on the bed. While my laptop boots up, I rub the bandage on my side. Torn intercostal muscle was the official diagnosis. Several weeks of hell, more like it.

Concentrate!

The ghosts, they sounded like they were in *The Brady Bunch* or *Scooby Doo*, using words like groovy. So, they were in college in the late 1960s or early 1970s. I type the sorority and San Antonio University into Google. A refined search of 1970 brings up the article I'm looking for. Take that, Rebecca. Found it in ten seconds, and she called me useless when it came to research.

San Antonio Tribune

November 13, 1972

Three female students from San Antonio University were found dead in and around their sorority house yesterday morning. Preliminary findings are unclear as to cause of death and whether it was suicide or homicide. Police are interviewing members of the community, the university, and the sorority. They are asking if anyone has any information to contact police headquarters immediately.

The article continues for three more paragraphs of nothing useful. Two weeks later I find the real story.

San Antonio Tribune

November 27, 1972

For once the actual story rivals the best Hollywood blockbuster in plotline. It's a story of greed, love, insanity, and death. A story that shows just how warped a human being can become until the word "human" seems to no longer apply. Had I not talked to the witnesses myself, I don't think I'd believe it could possibly be true—and yet here I am writing this article, wondering how I can ever reconcile these events in my psyche.

Three women in the prime of their lives, with everything to look forward to, are dead. Amy Terrence, Renee Becker, and Tracy Rodriguez are gone but will live on in infamy due to the horrendous crime committed against them. You've heard the phrase "publish or perish"? Well one assistant professor took that motto to terrible extremes on the night of November 11, 1972. In what can only be called insane, Dr. Jeffrey Rosenthal used a sorority for his ultimate psychological experiment. I wish I could say it was an experiment gone terribly wrong, but according to Dr. Rosenthal, everything went according to plan. "Better than I ever planned," he was quoted telling police.

Dr. Rosenthal started by seducing a young student, using every psychiatric trick in his arsenal to mold her into the perfect accomplice. From there he convinced her to aid him in an important study to help America win the cold war. By using love of him and love of country, he was able to completely control his unwitting accomplice into committing the most heinous of acts.

The stage was set: a high dose of LSD, a horror movie script, an adoring accomplice, and three innocent sorority sisters to play the victims. Even after reading his manifesto, I still don't understand what he was trying to accomplish from a scholastic perspective. But in Dr. Rosenthal's twisted mind, it all made a macabre sort of sense. Ply someone with LSD and a bit of fear, and they will do anything, reveal anything to stop the torment. He quoted CIA operation MKUltra as his inspiration, but the CIA denies the existence of such a program, so it remains nothing more than a conspiracy theory. They have also denied Dr. Rosenthal's claim that he was working on this project with funds provided by the government.

The police have not released the actual chain of events from that evening other than to reveal cause of death for the three victims. Amy Terrence fell down a staircase, breaking her neck. Renee Becker ran out into traffic and was struck by two cars. Tracy Rodriguez suffered the worst fate of the three. She was hacked to pieces, fingers, hands, then arms and left to bleed to death.

The tragic tale continues, but I have what I need. Three traumatized spirits haunting the site of their brutal murder. But why now? The spirit board may have called them forth, but that doesn't explain why they are so powerful...

9

Morning

KACIE

The chilly morning air feels invigorating against my heated skin as I step outside onto our front porch. Dad always keeps the house too warm in the winter. You'd think we lived in Alaska not San Antonio the way he cranks up the thermostat. Raising my face to the sky, I close my eyes and revel in the tiny drops falling in a mist around me. The scent of ozone fills the air, and I breathe deeply before licking moist drops from my lips.

Leaning against the wooden porch railing, I glance around the yard, noting the absence of my feathery familiars. Instead of bereft, their absence makes me feel good. I know they're over at Logan's house watching over my wounded friend. *Boyfriend.* That thought makes me smile. It's been eight weeks or so since we took our relationship from friends to more. There's just something about Logan that makes me feel... safe, understood, and special.

The soft flap of wings draws my attention to the sky. Poe soars down, landing on the railing beside my hands. He tips his head and gazes at me with curious eyes before releasing a small, cooing chirp. I run my fingers down the black feathers on his back, and he reacts like a cat, nuzzling against my hand.

"How is Logan?" I ask the large bird.

Poe jumps back and forth, then pecks at the downy feathers under his wing. *So much for open communication with my familiar.* Perhaps if things with the Circle ever quiet down for a week or two, I'll have time to read through some of the books Logan's mother recommended. As the high priestess of my Wiccan coven, she should be able to answer all of my witchy questions... yet that woman speaks more in riddles than anything coherent.

Poe's body becomes rigid, pulling me from my thoughts. I hear the roar of the engine before I see Daniel's SUV round the corner. The crow hops onto my shoulder as I head out to meet Daniel.

"Please don't tell me that bird is riding with us," Daniel says as I open the car door. "Go on, Poe. You can fly to Logan's much faster than I can drive there."

Poe hops onto the steering wheel and stares at Daniel. "I think that's an 'I'd rather ride'. Morning, Daniel." Poe waits for me to buckle my seatbelt before settling down on my lap.

"Strange, Cici… just strange. It's too early in the morning for more strange."

"More strange?" I ask as he pulls from the curb.

"I touched the spirit board last night and got a whole lot of strange." His hands grip the steering wheel hard enough to turn his knuckles white. "Then those three ghosts invaded my dreams."

Fear lances through me. "I—I didn't know that was even possible."

"Yeah, me neither."

"What—"

"It's bad. I only want to share once. Please… wait for the meeting."

"Sure." I glance at his pale face. Dark circles under his eyes attest to his lack of sleep. "You should've called me."

"There was nothing you could do," he says with a heavy sigh. "You were up half the night at the hospital with Logan. You didn't need my baggage on top of it."

"You don't have to deal with this stuff by yourself."

"I know—"

"No… I don't think you do." My hands ball up into fists. Poe chirps, trying to soothe my tension. "I was alone for so long, Daniel. It was awful. You have friends, you have the Circle. Use them. Let us support you when you need it. This lone wolf crap is starting to get real old."

"I don't—"

"You do. You keep us all at a distance with this charisma crap and all the jokes." I stare at him while he pulls to a stop in front of Logan's house. "Let us in."

"It's hard. I don't want to set myself up…"

"For a fall. I know. You and I have been in the same place. I'm telling you now… you will never be happy until you learn to trust again. I'm sorry about your father."

His stormy gray eyes meet mine, filled with raw pain. "He used me in a psych lecture again, as a lesson in delusion. God, Cici, once. I told him about my abilities once, years ago, and he won't let up on it. No matter how many psychiatrists I lie to, no matter… it's never good enough. He hates me."

I try to pull him into a hug, but he pushes me away. "Daniel…"

"Not now. Please, not now. We have a job."

"Okay."

He shoves the car door open and leaps from the driver's side like the seat is on fire. Poe lets out a loud *caw* and flies out, joining the other crows covering Logan's car. Though Daniel heads to the front door, I walk over to the Mustang. Sure enough, Logan sits behind the wheel, a dark scowl marring his face. Warmth floods me, along with a strong desire to comfort him. I softly rap on the window with my knuckles. He turns his head in a slow, deliberate movement, making me cringe inside. I'm not a morning person—dealing with two morose guys may be too much for me to handle…

at least not without a heavy dose of caffeine. A smile lights his face when he sees me peering in the window.

The grin turns to a look of chagrin as he opens the car door. "I know, I know. I can't drive. I just couldn't help myself."

"How you feeling?" I step back, watching him ease his way out of the low bucket seat, torn between helping and letting him do it himself. Refusing to play mother hen, I lace my fingers together.

"Your birds…" He slams the door shut. The crows covering the car flap their wings and ruffle their feathers but don't fly away. "They've been all over this car since yesterday and there's not one ounce of bird crap anywhere on it."

As if to emphasize Logan's words, several birds take flight, plopping their business all over the front lawn.

"Sometimes I think they understand us a bit too well." I glance at the dozens of bird eyes staring at me. "It's unnerving. And you didn't answer my question. How are you?"

"Better. The compression wrap cuts down on the rib pain, and the swelling in my knee is way down now."

"That's good," I murmur, leaning up to kiss his chin. The urge to hug him is so strong, but I nuzzle his neck instead to avoid hurting his side.

He wraps his arm around my shoulder. "Perhaps I should get you a leather jacket for Christmas." His fingers play with the collar of his jacket which I haven't returned since I borrowed it two months ago. He points to the arm holes which extend beyond my fingers to emphasize his point.

"I think I'll have to get one for you," I reply, wrapping my arms around my body. "I have no intention of returning it."

"You look adorable in my jacket." His lips brush my ear. A shiver courses through me from the light contact. He gazes over my shoulder, his mouth curling into a grimace. "Oh, crap. Please don't make me laugh. It hurts like a…"

"It isn't funny from where I'm standing," Daniel says from behind me.

I spin around and let out a short bark of surprised laughter. Poe is perched on top of Daniel's head, delicately pulling at the black strands of hair with his beak.

"Would it help if I told you he's trying to comfort you?" I bite my cheek to keep from doubling over in laughter.

"Hmm, that's a big no." Daniel crosses his arms over his chest. "Please do something before this giant bird decides to take a crap on my head."

"Come here, Poe," Logan says, holding out his arm. The crow flies from Daniel's head with a low *caw* and settles on Logan's forearm. "Need to talk?" he asks Daniel.

"Yeah, but later… at the meeting."

"He doesn't want to say it more than once," I add while stroking Poe's feathers. The action is soothing, akin to petting my dog, Kodiak, yet different. "We need to go." Poe takes to the sky, circling above us, while I take Logan's hand and lead him to Daniel's SUV.

10

Circle Gossip

LOGAN

What I thought was a blessing has quickly morphed into a curse. While I recline on the sofa with my injured knee propped up on a pillow, the girls surround me gossiping. It's the guys' turn to prepare the breakfast spread for the Circle, so they're all in the kitchen working while I relax. The smug smile leaves my face the moment the gossip turns to two Circle members.

"I walked in on something *interesting* last night," Rebecca says in a low voice.

"Share, share," Yolanda and Michelle chant in unison.

Rebecca glances at the kitchen before continuing. "Carl and I were over at Raven's researching the sorority ghosts." She pauses, staring at Raven who is arguing with Blake in the kitchen. "Blake was there, and he was fighting with Raven."

"Um, they fight all the time," Kacie says while fussing with the pillow behind my back. I could get used to this attention. "Nothing exciting there."

"No, I mean they were sparring in Raven's dojo." Raven comes from a whole family of hunters. Instead of a rec room, they have this awesome dojo.

Yolanda shakes her head, sending her multiple braids flying around her face. "Still nothing new. Those two train way too much."

Rebecca crosses her arms over her chest. "Shut it, they'll be back in a minute. Let me finish. Raven was using silver daggers, and she sliced Blake's arm."

"With silver?" Michelle's question comes out a mousy squeak. Being a werewolf, he's quite vulnerable to silver.

"Why would she use silver?" Kacie asks, her voice rising with each word.

"Shh, keep it down," Rebecca murmurs. "I haven't even gotten to the good part yet." She glares at the other girls, daring them to say anything else. "Okay, she went nuts—fussed over him like she cut it off. All traces of any animosity out the window."

"No way!" Yolanda says in a loud whisper.

"She tended the cut, then…"

After a long pause, I lose control, slapping my hand on the arm of the couch. "Then what?" The girls stare at me, startled by my sudden intrusion.

"She cradled his arm in her hands and kissed his bandaged forearm."

Silence. Deep, profound silence. Saying Blake and Raven fight like cats and dogs would be the understatement of the century. Odd. Before anyone manages a comment, Carl and Devon walk into the room, carrying trays of pastries and fruit.

Yolanda blows out a large puff of air. "What does that mean?"

"What does what mean?" Blake asks as he enters the room. His piercing, blue eyes take in the nervous titters and averted gazes of the girls. A small frown crosses his face which immediately changes to a bright, fake smile. He's wearing long sleeves, so I can't tell if his arm is still bandaged. "Talking about me again, eh? No worries, I'm used to being the elephant in the room… oops, I mean wolf."

"It's not like that, Blake," Kacie says, directing a glare at her silent friends. "Look you've only been with us for a few weeks. When I first joined, I can't count the number of times that conversation stopped when I walked into a room."

"So, princess, what were you all whispering about then? Hmm?" Blake's eyes narrow when Kacie remains silent. "Yeah, that's what I thought."

"We were worried about you and Raven," she blurts out amid startled gasps. "You've been working together a lot lately on this vampire thing, and the animosity between you guys is no secret…"

"It's fine, Kacie," Raven says, appearing from the kitchen with her arms folded across her chest. "It's a job, and I'll use whatever *tool* is necessary to complete the job."

Blake glances across the room at Raven—the hurt he's trying to hide with a blank expression apparent in his eyes. "Ouch, starshine. That hurt." His tone is light and joking. I don't know how the hell he manages it.

Raven's lips curl into a snarl. "I told you not to call me that, wolf boy."

"Breakfast is served!" Mrs. Kincaid says, stepping between the fuming pair. Her voice is cheerful, chirpy… just like my mother's when she's trying to diffuse a tense situation. "Everyone fill a plate. We have a very busy morning."

"Rebecca, why don't you start the meeting with an overview of your findings from last night," Mr. Kincaid says while the group is over filling their plates.

Kacie returns and places a plate of food on my lap. I must be predictable since she managed to pick out all my favorites, including a Boston Crème doughnut. When I smile at her in gratitude, her entire face lights up. My heart races. Damn that girl is gorgeous. She leans over and kisses my cheek before settling down beside me. She grabs the doughnut from the plate and brings it to her lips. Before taking a bite, she giggles and offers it to me instead. Though I'd rather kiss her senseless, I take a bite of the doughnut, wishing for the thousandth time that we were alone.

"Could you tone down the cuteness a little?" Raven asks as she settles on the chaise end of the sofa beside my elevated leg. "It's way too early, and there isn't enough caffeine in this house."

"Logan was assaulted by ghosts yesterday. I think he's earned a little TLC." Kacie sticks her tongue out at Raven before popping a glazed doughnut hole in her mouth.

"True, sorry," Raven mumbles, staring at the paper plate in her lap.

"If everyone's ready, I'll start," Rebecca says in her authoritative, take-no-prisoners tone.

"Actually, I have something I need to share first," Daniel says in a shaky voice. He crosses to the center of the room and leans against the brick fireplace. "I need to get this out before I lose my nerve." His arms fold across his chest as though trying to shield him from... something.

"Floor's yours," Rebecca says. She pats him on the shoulder and sits down beside Carl.

Carl sits up a bit straighter and puffs his chest out while watching for her reaction from the corner of his eye. When she doesn't seem to notice, he deflates a bit. Poor guy. He needs to be open with his feelings. I think he's been pining for Rebecca for two years now.

"I don't know where to start," Daniel says, pacing the floor. "It's really hard to talk about." He stops his restless movement and stares at the floor.

"You aren't on stage or giving a presentation in class," Kacie says, pushing up from the sofa. She takes Daniel's arm, leading him back to sit beside her. "Take a deep breath and relax. We're all here for you."

I'm completely torn. Part of me is so proud of her, of the care she shows my best friend. The other half is jealous of the attention Daniel is getting. The words of the spirits from yesterday echo through my mind. Lies. I know the spirits were lying, and yet... the way Kacie comforts Daniel makes my traitorous mind wonder. She turns to me with another one of her breathtaking smiles before resting her head on my shoulder. Yep, I'm a grade A jerk.

"Some of you know about my family, some don't. I'm going to mention it briefly because it's important to the situation last night." Daniel sinks back into the sofa—an unconscious attempt at hiding. "My dad is a world-renown psychiatrist in the field of schizophrenia and delusional disorders. Three... no four years ago, my abilities went a bit haywire. I thought he could help since he knew so much about the mind. I was young and scared and alone."

When he doesn't continue, Mrs. Kincaid says, "Psychic abilities do tend to wreak havoc at the onset of puberty."

"Yeah, no shit," Daniel says, scrubbing at his face with his hand. "I told my dad, and he thought I was nuts. I offered proof. Things I couldn't possibly know... but his mind was closed to the possibility. I was sent to shrink after shrink. My dad put me on some nasty anti-psychotic meds. After some awful side effects, which my father chose to ignore, I started flushing them. He still thinks I'm taking them."

Raven jumps to her feet. "That's sick. That, that's child abuse."

"Raven, you come from a family with abilities," Mrs. Kincaid says in her calm, soothing voice. Raven drops back to the sofa, drumming a staccato beat on the cushion. "Not everyone believes in psychic talent. To Dr. Westin, Daniel's abilities were a problem with his brain—a delusion. Continue, Daniel."

"I finally learned to pretend, to keep my powers to myself. But my father couldn't or wouldn't let it go. He would bait me, still does to this day, trying to get me to slip up. It's like he knows I'm lying. Maybe that's his psychic gift, a human lie-detector. It would explain lots of things in my past and also where I got my powers."

"I know that's one of my mom's powers," I say, rolling my eyes.

"Yeah, well, yesterday he used me again in a lecture at UTSA about delusions." Daniel sighs, a heavy, defeated sound. "He rehashed the whole lecture at the dinner table. Then had the gall to thank me for being so pathetic. His words, not mine."

"I'm sorry, Daniel, but your dad sounds like a prick," Blake says from his spot across the room. "I mean, who picks on their kids like that. It's wrong on so many levels."

Daniel rises and paces back and forth a few times. "Yeah, but that's beside the point. After dinner I was really upset, like wanted-to-throw-everything-in-my-room-against-the-wall upset. To distract myself, I pulled out the spirit board. Big mistake."

There are no more interruptions as Daniel continues to pace restlessly from the kitchen to the fireplace.

"There's nothing special about the board. The girls got it at the outlet mall. Just a standard issue game. My guess is one of them has spiritual power she's unaware of. Anyway, they managed to create a portal with the board, and our trio of vicious spooks came through."

"Do you know where the portal is?" Mrs. Kincaid asks.

"The portal is somewhere in the sorority house... but the board acts as a window. The sprits can travel through it," Daniel replies with a frown. "Weird, I know, but there it is."

"How do you—"

Daniel cuts off Mrs. Kincaid. "How do I know? Those spooks visited me last night. Tormented me. Endlessly." He turns away, staring at the fireplace. "Hours of hell. They knew everything... like they could read my mind or something. About my dad, my anxiety, and my fear." When he turns back to face us, I'm taken aback at the look of abject dread on his face. "They taunted me for hours. Told me my dad was going to lock me away in a loony bin. They knew my deepest fear, and they used it."

"They did the same thing to me," I murmur, meeting Daniel's sorrowful gaze. "I was in a bad place yesterday, because... well you know. They knew, and they used it against me. It was worse than the physical beating."

"What are you talking about?" Rebecca asks as she walks around gathering empty plates from everyone.

"I walked in on Daniel and Kacie kissing in the club room." I glance at Kacie, flinching at the hurt on her face.

"They were just rehearsing," Rebecca says like it should be obvious to everyone. Maybe it should've been.

"Yeah, well, they were all alone in the club room in each other's arms and I freaked. I'm not proud of it." The last sentence comes out a mumble.

"That's all beside the point," Kacie says, resting her hand on my thigh. "We have a trio of ghosts who have no qualms about physically and psychologically bullying anyone who crosses their path. We need to find a way to end this and soon."

A beep sounds from the other room, and Mr. Kincaid leaves without a word.

"Wait a minute. Those three had me pinned to a ceiling. They threw Logan into several walls. Why aren't you hurt?" Raven asks, giving Daniel a dark glare.

"Easy, Raven," Daniel says with a nervous chuckle. "The board may act as a window, but the spirits are still tied to the house where they died. They didn't have anywhere near the power they seem to have at home base. It's nice to know how you really feel about me, though."

"I didn't mean—"

"Do you have the board with you?" Rebecca asks, returning to her seat on the floor next to Carl. "Can we contact them?"

"Not a good idea," Mrs. Kincaid says. "I'd rather not introduce them to my house. They might decide to stay."

Silence fills the room while everyone considers our options. If we return to the house, we're risking life and limb—not to mention our psyches.

"I found out a bit about our ghosts last night," I say, breaking the long silence. "I sent the info to Rebecca, so I'm hoping she got more than I did."

"I sure did—"

Mr. Kincaid enters the room and cuts Rebecca off. "Okay, but before we continue with this case, I need to give out a new assignment. I just got word that the Austin Circle chapter is expecting Devon, Michelle, and Yolanda for the investigation at the Capitol building." The room erupts in loud grumbles. "It's bad timing, but you know how hard it can be to set up a nighttime investigation at a government building. This is a one-night-only deal. Figure out who or what is causing the nightly vandalism."

"Yes, sir," Devon says with a small salute. "We're on it. When are they expecting us?"

"As soon as possible," Mr. Kincaid replies, handing a small stack of paperwork to Devon. "I've already notified your parents, so you just need to go home for an overnight bag."

"I always miss out on the fun stuff," Yolanda mumbles. She grabs her purse, swinging it around in frustration. "I hope the Austin ghost is worth missing this drama."

Michelle snorts. "If it's even a ghost at all."

Devon, Michelle, and Yolanda walk out the front door to head to their new assignment. Silence fills the room again, the only noise the clacking of Rebecca's laptop keys as she works on her notes. Kacie pats my leg, then leaves to help clear the breakfast platters from the buffet table.

Leaning back, I try to melt into the sofa, wishing I could take a nap. I allow my mind to drift as I listen to the soft *click, click, click* of the laptop keys. Such a soothing sound... so rhythmic. A gentle tap on my arm jolts me back. Kacie hands me a couple ibuprofen and a can of Coke, along with a sweet smile. Morning light shines through the window, bathing her in an ethereal glow. Her red curls sparkle in the sun, glinting like newly-minted copper pennies. I swallow the pills while gazing up at my angel.

11

Insidious

~

KACIE

As I walk into the kitchen, a strange sensation creeps through me. My arms tingle, making the hair stand on end. The temperature drops. My breathy pants come out a soft misty fog in the sudden coldness. An invisible thread tugs at me, pulling me toward the side door. *Do I follow?* My bracelet pulses a warning, but I decide to ignore it.

Not wanting to risk losing the connection, I slip out the door before anyone notices. The energy is stronger outside. I follow it around the side of the house, feeling it pulse throughout my body. When I reach the front of the house, I'm drawn to Daniel's SUV. I run my fingers over the rear window. Energy crackles through my fingertips. Yanking my hand away, I cradle my sore fingers against my body. Poe lands on my shoulder, chattering at me in what sounds like a scolding.

"Kacie, what are you doing out here?" Blake yells from the porch. His voice sounds far away or maybe like he's shouting through a tube. I look at him, surprised at the distorted distance between us. "Forgive the pun, but you look like you've seen a ghost."

"They're messing with me." I glance back at the car window. "I think their power is growing. We need to stop them quickly before they have a chance to power up more."

A gust of frigid air plows into me, sending me flying backward. I skid along the asphalt road. Total déjà vu. The Foxblood Demon did this exact same thing to me two months ago. Do these ghosts know that? Did they pull it from my memories?

"Damn, princess." Blake kneels beside me on the street. He inspects my left arm which took the brunt of the fall. I guess I should've grabbed Logan's leather jacket on my way out. "Well, looks like some nasty road rash, but nothing some peroxide and bandages won't fix."

"They knew." Another cold chill courses through me. "How could they know?"

Blake hoists me into his arms with a gentleness that belies his werewolf strength. "What did they know?"

"Daniel and Logan were both terrorized by the spirits over something that deeply disturbed them." Memories flood my mind—the Foxblood Demon and his insidious plans for me. "They attacked me exactly the same way the Foxblood Demon did."

"Ah, that serial killer ghost I missed out on?"

"Yeah." I cuddle into Blake's warmth. Werewolves run hotter than humans, and right now I could use the heat. If a doctor told me ice water was flowing through my veins, I wouldn't be surprised.

"You're like a human icicle." Blake tightens his arms around my shaking body. He kicks the door open with his boot and carries me through.

"What the hell happened, Kacie?" Logan yells when we enter the room. "What possessed you to go outside alone?"

"Rhetorical question?" Daniel asks with a dry laugh. "I think we all know what or should I say who possessed her."

"Her arms are covered in road rash," Blake says as he sets me down on the sofa beside Logan.

"Road rash?" Carl's question comes out a tiny squeak.

"The spirits attacked her, sent her flying along the road," Blake replies, staring at Carl with a bewildered look. "Could someone get a first aid kit?"

"Already did," Mr. Kincaid says, kneeling down to inspect my arm. "Not as bad as last time." He pulls out the small pieces of asphalt with tweezers. "At least there aren't as many embedded rocks this time."

"Yeah, she mentioned last time too." Blake crosses his arms over his chest. "Anyone care to share just exactly what is going on here?"

"Those spirits invaded my mind," I reply, closing my eyes against the sharp pain as Mr. Kincaid continues to clean my arm. "I shut them out but not quickly enough. They picked up on the Foxblood Demon and my fear. I'll never forget what it felt like when he plowed into me… so much evil."

Shudders wrack my body, and Logan scoots closer with a small grunt of pain. He wraps his arm around my shoulders. "Shh, it's okay, baby," he coos in my ear. "I'm here. We're all here."

Tears burn my eyes, and I tamp down the memories, refusing to cry over that evil demon of a spirit. "I know. Just give me a minute. Those ghosts are really good at drawing out the memories and anguish associated with them."

"Tell me about it," Daniel mutters.

"Well they aren't ghosts so much as wraiths," Rebecca says, poking her head up from her laptop.

Carl scrunches his forehead. "I thought wraith was just the Scottish word for ghost."

"It is, sort of," Rebecca replies, shrugging. "I'd call these three revenants, but they weren't evil people in life as far as I know. A wraith is a ghost with malicious intentions. They typically feed on human fear and despair."

"What are revenants?" Carl asks.

"Irrelevant," Rebecca says, giving Carl a hard glare.

"No it isn't," Raven says, turning to Carl. "He needs to learn and it's a quick answer. A revenant is the spirit of an evil person. They strive to create havoc and destruction in life as well as death."

"So, the Foxblood Demon—"

Rebecca cuts off Carl's question. "No. See, it's never an easy answer with him."

Raven ignores her and continues the explanation. "The Foxblood Demon was an evil spirit, yes, but not a revenant. Revenants are mindless spirits bent on destruction. The Foxblood Demon was well aware of everything he was doing. He was a demonic spirit. I have a book you can borrow that explains this rather well."

"Thanks, Raven," Carl murmurs, looking like a dog that's been kicked too many times.

"Don't feel bad, Carl," Raven says. "I didn't know much about ghosts when I arrived a couple months ago. I just happened to finish that book last night."

"Well, if we're all done coddling Carl…" Rebecca trails off, her jaw clenched.

Something happened between those two. I peer around Mr. Kincaid who is still cleaning my arm. Rebecca glances at Carl from the corner of her eye. When she sees his hangdog expression, her face softens.

"Sorry, I'm going on no sleep," Rebecca says, patting Carl's leg.

"I'll get you a Coke." Carl jumps to his feet and races into the kitchen. He's back seconds later. "Here."

Rebecca's fingers brush Carl's as she takes the can from his hands. "Thanks."

Hmm, looks like I'll need to corner her later to find out what's going on with her and Carl. I always thought they'd make a great couple.

"Well, that about does it," Mr. Kincaid says, inspecting my arm. "The elbow took the brunt of it. Can you bend it?"

I bend it back and forth a few times, wincing at the sharp pain. "Maybe I'll take it easy for a day or two."

"Raven, will you wrap her elbow in a bandage while I clean up the mess?" Mr. Kincaid doesn't stop long enough to hear her answer. He gathers the bloody gauze and disappears into the kitchen.

"Rhetorical question, I guess," Raven mumbles as she winds the gauze around my arm. "Tell me if it gets too tight."

"Okay, so Logan and I both found some interesting info that should help," Rebecca says, her voice back to its normal cheerfulness. Oh, caffeine, the miracle worker. "So we know why the ghosts are gaining in strength. I mean a whole sorority to feed from would give them a big boost. What I couldn't figure out is why they came through so strong in the first place."

"It's odd, huh," I say, glad someone is finally voicing my concern. "Most ghosts are weak at first, gaining in strength as time passes."

"Hence the normal haunting progression," Rebecca says with a triumphant smile. "This case fits into my research so well. It's quite exciting really."

"Yeah, you hang out for a while pinned to a ceiling, then tell me just how awesome you think it is." Raven pulls the bandage too tight, and I hiss in a sharp breath. "Sorry."

"No, what I mean is the normal progression of a haunting." Damn, Rebecca's in lecture mode. "A family moves in. Weird things start: footsteps, banging, strange sounds. These tend to increase over time as the spirit grows in power until you have Armageddon, and they call us to help. I think the spirit needs time to charge. Many haunted houses sit vacant, so the spirit loses power over time."

"It's an interesting theory," Mr. Kincaid says. "But this current situation seems to refute your hypothesis."

Rebecca grins. "No, it just adds a mystery element which I think I may have solved."

"Are you going to share or just sit there with that stupid smirk on your face?" Daniel asks, pausing in his pacing circuit to stare at Rebecca.

"Geez, no patience. Okay, sometimes when we bless or smudge a house to rid it of hostile entities, they return… with a vengeance." Rebecca pauses again, glancing around the room. "Where do the hostile spirits go when we force them out?"

"The same place they all go," Daniel says, his voice tinged with irritation.

"Really?" Rebecca turns her gaze to me. "What do you think, Kacie?"

My fingers drum against my leg as I consider the possibilities. "Well, we send the willing spirits into the light, and from there they go... wherever they're supposed to, I guess."

"The light appears when a spirit is ready to move on," Logan adds, nodding.

"So if we banish an unwilling spirit, the light wouldn't appear." Rebecca's voice is triumphant. "So where does the spirit go?"

Daniel stops pacing and stares at Rebecca. "Purgatory?"

"Or something like that," Rebecca agrees. "So what if the spirits are trapped in limbo with nothing to do but practice and prepare for their revenge when released?"

"That's an awful thought," Raven says with a shudder.

"One ill-thought spirit board game or séance and wham—the return of a powerful, hostile ghost." Rebecca slams her laptop closed.

"Well, then we're kinda screwed," Logan says with a groan. "If we send those three back to... wherever... then the next time they come back who knows how strong they'll be."

"We have to convince them to let go of their anger and move on." The words sound even more ridiculous aloud than they did in my head before I spoke. "How?"

Rebecca rises from her seat on the floor. "I need to share their story, then we can figure out a way." She glances at the front door. "But first we need to do something about that spirit board. I don't want the hostiles listening to our plans."

12

Plans

~

LOGAN

After three long phone calls and a whole lot of arguing, we finally come to an agreement. The spirit board will be locked into a safe and lowered into Mr. Kincaid's pool. Our poor leader isn't overly happy with this solution, but our haunted relic expert said the metal combined with the deep water is the best way to keep the ghosts from using the board as another portal. Once the spirits are banished, then we can destroy the board. I watch from the patio as the others argue about how to lower the safe into the water with ropes. The thing must weigh a ton. Good thing we have a werewolf helping.

Blake releases a low growl, and the others scramble out of his way. Without pausing, he hefts the heavy safe in his arms and drops it into the pool. It floats on the surface for a few moments before sinking to the bottom.

The minute it sinks below the surface the air feels lighter. I breathe in a deep, cleansing breath, wincing from the pull on my ribs. The negative energy lifts, and the incessant buzzing in my ears ceases.

"Is it just me, or is it a lot easier to breathe now?" Raven asks, taking a loud breath through her mouth.

"Definitely a sensitive," Kacie says, nodding in agreement. "You may not see or hear spirits, but you can feel their energy."

"I don't know if that's good or bad." Raven tips her head, deep in thought. "I feel the energy of monsters too. I guess that's just my superpower."

"So, is it safe to talk about the ghosts now?" Rebecca asks, glancing between Kacie and me.

"You really don't feel any change in the air, do you?" I ask, wondering how she can be oblivious to such an obvious change in pressure.

"Nope, not a thing," Rebecca replies with a frown. "I can't decide if that's a good or bad thing."

"Our ghost friends are gone." I stare at the safe sitting at the bottom of the pool. "I suppose they've returned to the sorority house."

"Great, then I can tell you all about my research." Rebecca rubs her hands together, not in a nervous gesture but rather eager. Her excitement is a tad creepy. She disappears through the sliding glass door into the house. Before I can take a step, she pokes her head back out. "Are you coming or not?"

Kacie puts her arm around my waist and grins at me. Without a word, I allow her to assist me on the walk back to the family room. Though, truth be told, I don't need it. For some reason her actions fill me with warmth, and after the crap I've been through, I'm not ready to let go of that. After I'm seated at the sofa with my leg propped up, she leans down and kisses my forehead.

"Need any ice for your knee?" Kacie asks, brushing her fingers through the hair hanging over my left eye. "Maybe a haircut?"

"Ha, funny," I reply, shaking my head to move the hair back. "You love my hair like this."

"True. Ice?"

"No, I'm fine." I pat the sofa and she curls up against my side.

"Is everyone settled yet?" Rebecca asks in an exasperated tone. "Can I get y'all anything? Coffee, doughnuts, a paper?"

Carl lifts his hand in the air like a kid in class. "Actually, I'd like a Coke."

"Sarcasm, Carl. Learn it," Rebecca snaps at him. Then she stalks into the kitchen and returns with a can of Coke.

From the shocked expressions of my friends, I guess I'm not the only one thrown by her sudden kindness toward Carl.

"Logan, why don't you start," Rebecca orders, back to her commanding self. "You got the ball rolling."

"Yeah, sure." I sit up a bit straighter while organizing my thoughts. "I was in bed last night in pain, unable to sleep 'cause I didn't want the meds Dr. Hayes prescribed and something occurred to me. The ghosts all sounded like they were from an old episode of *Scooby Doo*. You know, like from the seventies. So I did some digging online and hit the jackpot."

The dull ache in my side turns into an annoying throb. When I squirm a bit, Kacie leans away looking sheepish.

"Sorry, forgot about your ribs," she whispers, scooting away.

"No, it's fine, really." I don't want to tell the whole Circle that I need the comfort but... "Can you switch to my other side?"

She switches places with Blake and leans gently against my side. Careful not to move too fast, I place my arm around her, resting it on her shoulders.

"Better?" she asks.

"Better. So, long story short, three girls were killed in and around that sorority house in 1972. The killer was an assistant psych professor who claimed he was conducting research. Our spirits names are Amy, Renee, and Tracy. The professor was either trying to replicate the CIA's MKUltra experiment or working for them— not sure. He dosed the three women with dangerous levels of LSD then played horror movie with them.

Amy fell down the stairs and broke her neck while running away in terror. Renee ran out into traffic in front of the house in a panic-fueled fugue and was hit by two cars. Tracy... well she was hacked to bits by a meat cleaver or something."

"No wonder those spirits are so angry," Raven says, wrapping her arms around her chest. "What an awful way to die."

"It gets worse." I lace my fingers with Kacie's when she reaches for my hand. "The professor first seduced another woman from the sorority and used her as an accomplice. That's how he was able to orchestrate the whole sordid thing. He used mind control techniques you only hear about in conspiracy theories and horror movies. The poor woman was warped completely to his will."

Blake leans forward, resting his elbows on his knees. "He didn't kill her too?"

"No. And I couldn't find anything about her identity either. I called Rebecca and passed everything on, then gave in and took a pain pill. Slept like the dead."

"Am I the only one who's never heard of MKUltra?" Kacie asks.

Raven shakes her head. "Nope. No idea what he's talking about."

"MKUltra was a conspiracy theory until documents were released in the eighties," Carl says, practically bouncing in his excitement. "The CIA, DOD, and other government agencies subjected unsuspecting US citizens to mind control experiments starting sometime in the 1950s. One of the favored methods was dosing a person with LSD and studying their reactions to it. They also used sensory deprivation, hypnosis, mental torture, all sorts of ugly things in an attempt to gain control of another human being. They believed that by dosing someone with LSD and altering their reality, they could alter their entire perception. Weird shit, if you ask me. These tests went on up until the early seventies. It's possible the professor was involved in some way. The government routinely employed psychiatrists for the project."

"Wow, just wow," Raven says, her eyes wide. "Are you sure this isn't just a conspiracy theory? It seems absurd that the government could use us as test subjects without our consent."

"The fifties were a different time," Mr. Kincaid adds. "The cold war, the threat of nuclear annihilation, and the red scare created an air of desperation. The US was anxious to stay one step ahead of the Soviets any way possible. Things were sanctioned that should never have been considered in the first place."

"Okay, so this professor used a combination of the MKUltra techniques to seduce the girl, then decided to use her to help him run some sick experiment at the sorority house?" Kacie's body stiffens beside me as she speaks. Her hand clutches my arm. "How could someone be so... so..." Her voice trembles, and I pull her tight enough to send a sharp pain shooting through my side.

Raven finishes Kacie's sentence. "Despicable? Contemptible?"

"You know, I originally managed to get by on the assumption that the girl he seduced was weak." Rebecca's voice is soft, forlorn. "But she was just like me. I-I figured out who she was based on sorority photos, school records, and court records—illegally obtained." She glances at Mr. Kincaid. "Sorry."

"I'll pretend I didn't hear it," he replies, his mouth set in a grim line.

"Anyway, her name was, or rather is, Angela Baxter. She was an honor student, top in her class, pre-med, active in both high school and college. When she met Professor Rosenthal, she was a sophomore…" Rebecca trails off, staring at her laptop like it might hold the answer she seeks. "It makes no sense. Why would a smart girl like that fall for tricks and seduction? We—I mean she—should have known better."

"Wait a minute," Raven says, a look of shock on her face. "This woman is still alive?"

"Yeah, she was placed in a psych ward for ten years after she testified at the trial," Rebecca says, twirling a strand of brown hair around her finger. "When she was released, she never married, had kids or a career. Just a string of odd jobs. Her life was ruined… she was destroyed."

"What happened to the loony professor?" Blake asks, poking at Rebecca with his foot.

Her head snaps up, and she glares at him. At least that's better than her earlier despair. "He was found guilty on three counts of murder one, along with drug charges and kidnapping. He was executed by lethal injection in 1983."

"That answers one question," I say, breaking a long silence. "We know why the spirits are so angry. But why are they so powerful?"

"I have a theory on that as well," Rebecca replies, snapping her laptop closed. "In 1998 the Orion Circle did a cleansing of the place. According to the file, they were unable to convince the spirits to move on and had to force them out. After three blessings and several smudgings, the activity ceased. But that was just your ordinary sentient haunting: footsteps, voices, things moving around. They did manifest at times and scare the crap out of the residents, but nothing like what they're doing now."

Kacie clears her throat. "The spirit board brought them back. But from where?"

"Purgatory? Limbo?" Rebecca pauses, her forehead furrowed in thought. "Like I said before, I think they go somewhere in between. Someplace where they have nothing to do but plot their return."

"So, Logan was right. We can't force them out or they could return again even stronger," Raven says with a visible shiver.

"We need to cross them somehow," Kacie says in a small voice. "Cross three nasty, powerful spirits."

"That's your specialty, Cici." Daniel glances at her with a sympathetic look. "Any ideas?"

"Actually, yes, I have a good one."

13

Lesser of Evils

~

KACIE

Snaking my hand across the backseat, I grab Logan's hand, lacing our fingers together. He squeezes my hand, and I glance up at him, losing myself in his eyes. But the moment passes quickly. His grin fades at my grim expression. When he opens his mouth to speak, I shake my head. I don't want to talk about this madness now. After all, this field trip was my idea. How can I possibly walk up to a sixty-year-old woman and ask her to relive the event that ruined her life.

It's not fair.

Life isn't fair. I can hear Dad's words in my mind clear as day. It was his answer to my preteen-angst tantrums. It didn't take long for me to stop saying those words. As if sensing my thoughts, my phone vibrates. A text from Dad.

Have you decided?

I pull my hand from Logan's with a pang of regret. *No.* I text back, hoping he'll let it go. No such luck.

It's only a few days. Try.

Damn. I can't deal with this right now... not with three angry ghosts who relish using our inner turmoil against us.

"What is it?" Logan asks, resting his hand on my thigh. His fingers play with the new hole formed from my skid across the pavement this morning.

"He wants me to make a decision about *her.*"

I don't elaborate. Logan knows my estranged mother wants to come visit for a weekend. She bolted, left me behind without a word or a glance, unable to deal with my abilities. It's only been two months since I discovered she had powers of her own. Sure her vision gave Logan the info he needed to save us from the Foxblood Demon. And, yeah, she apologized for leaving. But still...

"I don't know if I want to see her... you know, let her in again." My tone is soft, timid, the hurt plain in each syllable.

My phone vibrates again, this time a call. Logan gently takes the phone from my tight grasp.

"Hi, Mr. Ramsey," he says. It's so quiet in the car, I can hear my dad's voice but can't make out the words. "We're on our way to interview a client in a rather emotionally-charged case. Would it be okay to discuss this issue with Kacie tonight?"

I glance over at Logan, a smile tugging at my lips despite my foul mood. He always sounds so formal when dealing with my father. It's rather amusing. Dad talks for a minute or two—a long time for a yes.

"I'll talk to her, sir," Logan says, nodding his head. "Thanks." He hands the phone back, and I lay it down on the seat between us.

"Talk to me about what?" I ask, already aware of the answer.

"What else? Your mother of course." He takes my hand, squeezing it tight. "I'll be there with you, so will my mom. I think you might regret it if you don't at least try."

"Maybe," I reply, cringing at my lost, pathetic tone. The fact that my mother makes me feel like this is reason enough to avoid her. And yet... "Maybe you're right. I'll talk to Dad tonight. But, I need to put my problems aside right now and focus on the case."

"Good idea," Rebecca says from the front seat. So that's why she and Daniel were so quiet. They were listening to every word. "The whole Circle will be there for you, Kacie. We'll be your support when you deal with your deadbeat mom. Ms. Baxter will have no one but us... at least according to my research. Her parents are dead, she was an only child... she never married or had any kids of her own. How lonely..."

"Do you have a plan, Cici?" Daniel asks. Our eyes meet in the rearview mirror.

I shake my head. "Time is short. I'm going all in with the truth."

"Are you sure that's a good idea?" Rebecca asks, glancing over her shoulder. She and Logan exchange a look I can't decipher. "She might not believe in ghosts. And even if she does, this story is… well… rather fantastic."

"We'll have to make her believe," I say, refusing to back down. "Logan has a way of convincing people. We'll let him take the lead. After all, he did convince my dad to open his mind."

"I don't know whether to thank you or not." Logan caresses the back of my hand with his thumb. "This isn't something I'm looking forward to."

"All we can do is try." Raising our joined hands, I place a tender kiss on his fingers.

"Yeah, let's hope for the best," Rebecca agrees. Her head flops against the headrest. "Okay, quick brief before we arrive. Ms. Baxter is sixty-three. She's been in and out of psych hospitals since the event. When her parents died, she came into a ton of money and moved into a retirement community. It's been over ten years since her last hospitalization. I'm afraid we're going to send her right back to the loony bin."

"Or we could provide the closure she needs to move on with life," Logan says. "I think she's been lonely and confused… not to mention scared her entire life. Maybe confronting these spirits will help her find peace."

"See, I told you he's good," I say, unable to contain my grin.

Rebecca laughs. "Yeah, yeah, he could sell brimstone to a demon."

"I'm fuzzy on the details," Daniel says over Rebecca's laughter. "I don't want foot in mouth disease, so give me the quick version of events."

"Foot in mouth disease?" Rebecca asks, biting her lip. "Where did you pick that up?"

"From Mr. Kincaid." Daniel glares at Rebecca. "He says I have a tendency to suffer from it."

"True." I pat Daniel's shoulder. "But we love you anyway."

"I don't know how much Ms. Baxter actually remembers from that night. Hopefully not much…" Rebecca trails off and stares out the passenger window. "It must have been awful, terrifying, surreal." She leans her forehead against the glass. "Ever since Logan called me, and I started researching this… this… hell, I don't even know what to call it."

"Massacre," Daniel murmurs.

"Yeah, basically. From what I gathered, Ms. Baxter was dosed with LSD that night, so it was probably more of a nightmare than reality." She releases a heavy sigh. "No, more like a nightmare come to life. It would be bad enough to witness the torture and murder of your three best friends, but to be under the effects of LSD… I just can't imagine. She was at the trial, even called as a witness, but she didn't make it through the entire trial."

"Why?" Logan asks.

"She broke down, complete mental disassociation. I guess hearing what actually happened from the prosecution was just too much for her. Didn't matter though, it was basically an open and shut case."

"So how do we keep her from breaking again?" Logan asks as he drums nervous fingers on the armrest.

"We can't," I say in a whisper. "All we can do is hope she wants to help her friends enough that it keeps her from falling apart."

Daniel bangs his hand on the steering wheel. "This sucks!"

"No shit," Rebecca agrees.

14

Angela

~

LOGAN

My finger hovers over the doorbell, refusing to move the extra inch or so needed to push the button. This poor woman has probably spent her whole life recovering from that one traumatic time. Where the hell do I get off coming here to dredge it all back up? Kacie's fingers close around mine, and she leans into my back.

"Ms. Baxter needs closure too," she whispers. "I know this will be hard for her, but what choice do we have. She is part of this whether she wants to be or not."

Kacie's words firm my resolve, and I poke the doorbell—probably a bit harder than necessary. Seconds pass. It's a small apartment in a retirement community... it shouldn't take this long for the woman to answer the door. Just as I'm hoping she isn't home, I hear shuffling on the other side of the door. It flies open, revealing a woman who looks as though she wears every one of her sixty-three years on her face. Deep lines surround dark, hardened eyes that glare at us. Her hair falls to her shoulders in a mass of messy, out of control, silver curls. Twin gray-and-black spotted cats swirl around her bare legs sticking out from beneath a garish floral muumuu. I blink a few times. She looks like the epitome of the crazy cat lady.

"I'm not buying whatever it is you're selling," she says before closing the door.

"Wait, please," Rebecca says, placing her hand on the door to stop it mid-swing. "Are you Ms. Baxter?"

"What's it to you?" the woman asks, her eyes narrowing in suspicion.

"Please, ma'am, we need to talk to you," I say in a soft, gentle tone, like I'm talking to a skittish dog. Before I can continue, both cats cross the threshold to wind their tails around my legs, while brushing their faces against my jeans.

"Well, if Samson and Delilah think you're okay, then I suppose you can all come in," she says, stepping back from the doorway. "Animals are good judges of character. In all the time I've had them, you're the only person those cats seemed to show any interest in. Odd."

Odd indeed. I reach down and stroke the backs of both cats. They stare up at me with matching pale, blue eyes. Knowing eyes... cats always seem too intelligent for their own good.

"I know who y'all are," Ms. Baxter says without turning as she leads us into a small sitting area. "Go ahead sit down. I've been expecting you."

"Um, how?" Rebecca asks as she sits on a faded, floral sofa. "How could you know we were coming when we didn't until about an hour ago?"

"Saw it on the news, I did." Ms. Baxter settles into a peach armchair, propping her slippered feet on the matching ottoman.

"What did you see on the news?" I ask, wandering around the small room. Only a few steps between the sofa and the fireplace. Not enough room to pace, and I really feel the need right now. Sitting hurts a whole hell of a lot worse than standing, even with my messed up knee.

Ms. Baxter glances at each of us with an odd expression. "My old sorority house, the prank, the circus tent, all of it. You *are* with the Orion Circle, right?"

"Yes, we are. I'm Rebecca Travers, the lead investigator. This is my team—Daniel Westin, Logan Finley, and Kacie Ramsey," Rebecca says, narrowing her eyes. "What do you know about us?"

"Everything," Daniel says before Ms. Baxter can answer. His face is ashen, and he crosses his arms over his chest. "Sorry, I thought it quicker this way." He nods to the coffee cup sitting on the table beside Ms. Baxter's chair. "She's been waiting for hours."

"Well, I guess that makes this easier, then," Rebecca says, letting out a deep breath.

"No, it doesn't." Daniel tips his head, scowling at her. "She has no intention of helping us."

"Now see here, young man." Ms. Baxter shakes her finger at Daniel. "I don't know where you get off pulling some psychic reading on me, but I—"

"See my friend over there?" Daniel points at me leaning against the fireplace mantel, trying to take some weight off my swollen knee without scrunching up my sore ribs. "Those ghost friends of yours attacked him yesterday. Threw him into several walls. Put him in the hospital. They also pinned another friend to the ceiling in that sorority house. We don't have time for games, subtleties, or niceties."

"But, how can she know?" Rebecca asks. "I mean we only came up with this plan an hour ago."

"She's an intuitive," I say, leveling a hard glare at Ms. Baxter. "She read us the moment we walked through the door... with the help of her familiars."

The twin spotted cats, sit on either side of my legs, still as statues. When those inscrutable cat eyes meet mine, they stare at me as if to say, *took you long enough.* They release a simultaneous, *meow.*

"I'm sorry, kids, but this has nothing to do with me." Ms. Baxter waves her hand in a dismissal. "Banish the ghosts like the last group from the Orion Circle did."

"Yeah, well there's a problem with that." I limp across the room to tower over the glowering woman. Her attitude is not what I expected, especially given that she's a witch. *Where the hell is her sense of responsibility?*

"If you think to intimidate me, I'd think twice," she says with a dark, humorless laugh. "You look like a light breeze would knock you over right now, boy."

Daniel moves to her right, and she shakes her finger at him. "No closer. I know what your psychic power is. Psychometry. Am I right?"

"I prefer clairsentient," Daniel says, sticking his hands up his sleeves. "Unarmed, see?"

"Where do spirits go when they're banished from our plane?" Kacie asks from her seat on the edge of the ugly sofa. "I mean, demonic spirits go to Hell... I think. But what about the other spirits, the ones who just refuse to leave?"

"Why would I care?" Ms. Baxter asks in a bored, yet frustrated tone.

"Because three of your friends are suffering," Kacie says. Though her voice is neutral, calm even, she doesn't bother to hide her hands clenched into tight fists. "They died in such terror. The afterlife must have been so confusing. I mean they didn't move on, but the Circle wasn't called out until years after their deaths. Do they feel the same terror in an endless loop?"

Ms. Baxter folds her hands in her lap. "I-I never really thought about it."

"No, you did think about it," I say in a soothing tone. "You thought about it constantly, and it almost broke you. We've read your files. You've been in and out of psych wards for years."

"It's my fault," she whispers, dropping her head, so her long curls hide her face. "All of it… my fault."

"It isn't your fault," I reply, crouching before her. Crap. I forgot about my knee. The painkillers worked… at least they did before I went and did something stupid. I plop down on my butt to alleviate the pain radiating from my knee. "How could any of this be your fault?"

"I'm an intuitive, a sensitive… that bastard, Jeffrey… I never guessed." Her voice breaks as she sucks in a gasped breath. "How could I not sense the evil in him? I led my three best friends to slaughter because I was too starry-eyed-in-love to see the monster inside."

"Ms. Baxter—"

"Angela, call me Angela," she says cutting off Rebecca. "The Ms. just reminds me that I'm alone."

"Um, Angela… I did some research last night on Jeffrey Rosenthal." Rebecca pulls a thin file from her messenger bag. "Did you know that he was placed in a special soundproof room at the prison for the criminally insane? Not only that but he still almost escaped six times. Six. Then during the trial… the DA's notes indicated that he seemed to hold the jury in some sort of thrall when he testified. The defense attorney wanted Jeffrey to issue the closing remarks, but fortunately the judge refused to allow it. Though he never managed to escape prison after his sentencing, he did manage to escape his cell several times. And those were just the incidents I found in articles on the internet. Who knows how many times he came close to escape before they put him in solitary confinement. He stayed in solitary until his execution."

"I don't understand…" Angela looks up, her eyes filled with raw hope. "He was… special?"

Rebecca hands the file to Angela. "We have a doctor in the Circle who carries the power of persuasion. I think Jeffrey Rosenthal did as well."

"Shit," I murmur under my breath. "Then we're lucky he was convicted and executed. Do you think the doc could talk herself out of arrest and conviction?" Dr. Hayes makes me nervous. I've seen her use her power of persuasion on a hardened police detective. He turned into a docile pussycat with just a gentle suggestion. Scary.

"I remember when he spoke, the entire class would hang on his every word," Angela says, leaning forward in her chair. "Just like I am now… leaning forward… eager for every word he uttered."

"Yes, he definitely had some power," Rebecca says, nodding. "We'll never know the full extent of his *gift* thankfully."

Angela doesn't seem to hear her, completely lost in her memories. "When he called me aside after class, I was so excited, proud, eager to do anything to help with his research. I felt honored that he chose me out of hundreds of students. Me." Her shoulders slump. "Little did I realize he was just using me." She looks up, her eyes pleading… I guess for understanding…

maybe. "His research was fascinating. He made it that way. By the time he brought up using my sorority sisters as guinea pigs, I was already so far under his spell—it seemed a perfectly normal request. Why didn't my power protect me?"

"I don't think we'll ever know the answer to that question," I say, meeting her desperate gaze. "I really wish I had the answers… but I don't. Psychic powers are unpredictable at best. Wiccan powers more so."

"I didn't become a practicing Wiccan until thirty years ago." Her gaze moves to the two gray cats. "Samson and Delilah found me back in the mid-eighties or so. Egyptian Mau is their breed. Very rare. I felt their power as familiars immediately."

"Those cats are over thirty years old?" Kacie asks, her eyes widening as she watches the cats strut around, their tails twitching in the air.

"You don't have to believe me, but yes they are." Angela pats her lap and both cats jump up simultaneously. "Familiars are magic, so their lifespans can be tied to lots of different things… but most common is the witch or warlock they're tied to."

"So, I could have Poe and his flock for the rest of my life?" Kacie's gaze flies to the window where Poe is perched watching us.

"The crow is yours," Angela says with a snort. "I thought it an ill omen when he seemed so interested in us. I'm glad he's your familiar instead."

"How will I ever explain a flock of birds following me everywhere?" Kacie drops her face into her hands, making me chuckle. She has a tendency toward melodrama—must be the actress in her. "Glad you think this is funny."

I bite my lip and try to keep a straight face. "Sorry."

She peeks out at me between her fingers, a brash grin on her face. "You're so easy." Her laughter drops the tension level in the room. I hadn't realized how stifling the air had become.

"All joking aside," Rebecca says while digging through her messenger bag. "We have a problem, and we need your help, Angela."

Angela straightens in her chair. "No."

"No?" Rebecca's voice carries her shock, along with a touch of bewilderment.

"I'm not going back to that house, and I'm not facing the ghosts of my friends," Angela says shaking her head and her hands emphatically. "No way. I can't. I won't."

"You have no choice," Rebecca says, narrowing her eyes into her evil glare. "You are the only person who has a chance to help them move on."

"I don't care," Angela replies in a clipped tone.

"Do you know what happens to spirits who don't move on?" Kacie asks, continuing her previous line of questioning. No one answers. We all know the question was for Angela specifically. "Angela, do you know?"

"Of course not," Angela finally replies. "No one can."

Kacie tips her head. "Haven't you ever wondered?"

"Stop trying to lead me somewhere and just spill it."

"When they're here—sentient spirits—they still seem to feel the pain they felt in life," Kacie says. "They have memories. It's like they only lost their corporeal body."

"You can't—"

Kacie cuts of Angela's interjection. "I'm a powerful physical medium, so yes I can know. For over forty years, your three friends have suffered when they should have found peace. They will continue to suffer unless you help them."

"I already told you—just banish them like the last Orion Circle group did."

"Well, see that's a problem," I say with a dry laugh. "We don't know where they went when they were banished, but we do know they came back angry as all hell and stronger."

"What do you mean?" Angela's gaze darts between us.

"They hurt us physically—Daniel told you that earlier." I try to push up from the floor, but between my ribs and my knee, I'm stuck. Daniel and Kacie rush to my side and help me stand. I glare down at Angela. "You can't stick your head in the sand on this one. Your ghost friends have gone rogue and are in danger of becoming demonic spirits."

"Is that even possible?" Angela asks as the color drains from her cheeks.

"I don't know," I reply, trying to keep from yelling. My frustration with this woman has hit its peak.

"They're your friends, shouldn't you care more?" Kacie asks, probably feeling my frustration. I send her a glance as a silent thank you. I need to keep my cool if I'm to continue playing good guy.

"Whether it's possible or not is immaterial," Rebecca says, slamming a file down on the coffee table. She smirks when Angela jumps about a foot in her chair. "They are wreaking havoc at the sorority house. They are a danger to everyone in that general area. If we banish them, they'll go back to Purgatory—or whatever, and the next time they find a crack to squeeze through back into our dimension, they may be too powerful to stop."

"Well, regardless, it's not really my problem anymore," Angela says, lowering her gaze to the floor. "I've been through a lot more than any of you can ever imagine. No more."

"They need you," I say, looking down at her bowed head. "They are all alone, scared, twisted. If they become demonic ghosts, they could spend the rest of eternity in torment."

"You don't know that!" She glares up at me, her eyes angry slits.

"No, I don't," I concede. My nostrils flare as I try to maintain control of my temper. "But neither do you.

They need to go into the light to have any chance of salvation. And you are their last hope."

"I don't know how." Her voice is barely a whisper.

"We'll help," I say before she can add anything else. "We'll be with you the entire time. Come Hell or high water, we'll be there. We'll help you save your friends."

15

Back to the Lions' Den

~

KACIE

Against the odds, Logan maneuvered Angela into a corner until she was forced to help or to admit she didn't care. Uncomfortable doesn't begin to describe the overall mood in the SUV. Sandwiched between a seething Logan and a terrified Angela, I take slow breaths in an attempt to quiet my racing heart. When I reach out to grab Logan's hand, a cat head butts it away. My eyes narrow as I meet the possessive gaze of the Egyptian Mau cat perched on Logan's lap. The other watches from the floor at Logan's feet, bright eyes glinting from behind his calf. It appears Logan may finally have the familiars he's wanted for such a long time.

Shaking my head, I scratch the cat in his lap behind the ears until it lets out a loud purr. When it looks away,

I take Logan's hand, lacing our fingers together. The cat glares down at our entwined hands before turning his gaze to the blurred landscape outside the car window. It will be interesting to see how the cats react to Poe and his flock.

Angela remains silent as she stares out the passenger window, her knuckles white from clenching the handle on the door frame. I want to say something encouraging or reassuring but can't think of anything. Instead I lean into Logan's side.

"Are you ready to open?" I ask in a hushed whisper. Normally before entering a site, we prepare ourselves to communicate with the spirits. Quiet meditation and deep breathing to open the lines of communication.

"Do you think it's a good idea? I don't want to open myself up to those ghosts again... and I don't think you should either."

"Noted." I snuggle against his side when he puts his arm around my shoulders, pulling back a bit when he cringes. "Sorry."

"It'll take some getting used to." He leans down and kisses the top of my head. "Promise me you'll be careful in there."

"Really? I think it's me who should be telling you that," I say, squeezing his hand. "Are you sure I can't convince you to stay outside?"

"Those ghosts have nothing on me today," he murmurs, a look of defiance gleaming in his eyes. "I got it all out yesterday. You and Daniel are my best friends, and I trust you both. You, on the other hand, have something they can use against you."

"My mother."

"Yep." He caresses my thumb with his. "I don't suppose you'd agree to remain behind."

"I already know that my mother is a deadbeat, selfish woman who abandoned me when I needed her most," I say, trying to keep the hurt from my voice.

"Mmm, Cici, you have no idea how they'll take your thoughts and manipulate them until you can't see straight," Daniel says without taking his gaze from the road. "I thought I'd come to terms with my father until those three bitches came calling."

"I'll be fine," I bite out, angry that my mother is causing problems from all the way in Arizona through her mere existence.

"I hope so, 'cause we're here," Rebecca says, a tiny tremor in her voice. "The extermination tent is downright creepy."

Silence fills the car as Daniel pulls the SUV up the driveway beside the tent-covered house. The red-and-white tent sticks out—a garish display on the otherwise quiet residential street dotted with normal houses. As I step out of the car, I take a few deep breaths, testing the air for the heaviness of dark energy. The air is still, so quiet, but my bracelet dances to a rhythm of its own. Poe settles down on the bumper of the SUV, his dark eyes regarding the two cats winding around Logan's legs. They seem to come to a mutual agreement as there is no loud cawing or angry hisses. Poe takes flight, soaring to land on the edge of the tent near the front porch.

"Rebecca, you need to stay out here," Logan says when she starts across the dry grass.

"But—"

"You are our link to the outside world." He pauses as the cavalry arrives in the white Circle van. "I trust your judgment. If you think things are beyond our abilities, send in Raven and Blake to get us out."

"Okay." Rebecca plops down, the dry grass crunching around her. "You have an hour, or until all hell breaks loose… whichever comes first."

"We go in as a united front," Logan says, taking my left hand and motioning for Daniel to take my right. "We are stronger together. Kacie, you can pull on my energy as well as Daniel's. We are here to support you and protect Angela."

I take Daniel's hand, oddly glad that it's as sweaty as mine. Nerves I guess. We walk through the brittle grass, probably looking ready to play a game of Red Rover or something. Angela follows behind us, so close I can hear her quick breathing in the eerie silence. A wicked cackle breaks the stillness, sending a chill through me. Daniel, Logan, and I present our united front, staring at the tent rippling near Poe. He screeches, flying off the tent to circle our heads, still *cawing* his displeasure. His calls sound like a warning, a siren I know we should heed. The two cats approach the tent, their backs arched, and their fur fluffed. They hiss at the tent in unison before turning tail and running back to the SUV.

"Don't run, Angela," Logan says without looking over his shoulder. "These three feed on fear. You have to swallow it and move forward with us."

"I'm fine," she says in a steady tone. "I'm ready to do this. It's time for all four of us to move on."

"Take my hand," Daniel says, holding his right hand out to Angela.

"We're ready," I call out to Blake, standing near the tent flap.

He nods, then bends over and slices through the zip ties holding the fabric closed. When he slices through the last tie, the flap flies open, hitting him in the face.

"Call me if you need me," Blake says, grabbing the fluttering tent with both hands. "Remember, I have great hearing. I'll hear you even if it's just a whisper." The last sentence is directed toward Angela.

"Were..." Angela trails off waiting for an answer.

"Wolf, yes."

"Good to know," Angela says, seemingly unfazed by his admission. I suppose with her odd familiars, she's probably well-acquainted with the supernatural world.

"Be careful." Blake pulls the tent higher so we can enter. "It's awfully quiet in there."

"We're hoping this encounter is anticlimactic," Logan says as he leads us through the open front door.

"You hoped wrong." A feminine voice cackles, ringing through the hallway.

Daniel's hand is ripped from mine as he flies into the wall behind us. Frigid winds batter me, sending my hair swirling around my head. My fingers tighten around Logan's hand, and I brush the hair from my eyes with my forearm. Electricity crackles in the air around us. Tiny goosebumps crop up on my arms. Logan's aura brushes against me, a feather-like, tickling sensation. The moment our auras merge, the heaviness in the air vanishes, and I take a deep breath. I push my aura outward until it envelopes Daniel and Angela where they fell to the floor.

"What is this?" one of the ghosts asks in a scratchy tone, like she'd gargled glass. She pokes at our psychic barrier with an ethereal finger but is unable to penetrate it.

"Thanks." Daniel pushes to his feet. He holds his hand out to Angela and pulls her from the floor. "You okay?"

Angela nods, her eyes wide. "Yeah. Surprised, but okay."

"Don't ignore me!" The loud shriek hurts my ears, but I pretend to find something immensely interesting on my nails. A painting flies from the wall, crashing next to my feet. I swallow down my scream and clench my teeth. "Stop it! Stop ignoring me."

"That's a rather ugly painting, don't you think?" Daniel says, bending over to inspect the broken masterpiece. He runs his fingers along the canvas. "Art student, 1989, really full of herself. No heart in this piece at all."

One of the spirits materializes inches from his face. Even with the years of acting, I'm still impressed when Daniel fails to react to her silvery presence. As far as I'm aware, Daniel can't see the colorful energy of our protective auras. His trust bolsters my belief in my own abilities.

"Normally when I touch art, I can feel the emotions of the artist." He pauses, straightening back up. The spirit follows his every move. "This one, there's nothing but precision, like paint by numbers."

"You. Will. Not. Ignore. Us!" The three spirits scream in unison, sending a whirlwind battering against our shield.

Logan raises a hand, not speaking until the wind around us dies down. "I understand you are angry and hurt and maybe confused. We are here to help you, but we won't unless you calm down and talk to us."

The spirit circling Daniel moves to tower over Logan, her visage changing from translucent silver to dark gray. Her form warps until it has the appearance of a tall, twisted shadow person. But she isn't a demonic, inhuman shadow. She is still the spirit of a young woman, murdered in a heinous fashion, then banished from our plane. It's eerie, though, seeing her take this demented form—I wonder if she knows this is what might be in store for her if she continues to embrace her rage and hatred. I always wondered if shadow people were ever human spirits... now I think I know the answer. Maybe they were human spirits who couldn't let go of their past life and finally went insane, allowing evil to consume them.

"No, not today," I mumble under my breath.

"Huh?" Logan asks with a quizzical look.

I shake my head. "Just thinking aloud... about the origin of shadow people."

"We brought someone who wants to talk to you," Logan tells the dark spirit creeping up the wall to the ceiling. "She wants to help. But you need to calm down enough to share your story. Tell us what happened to you. Why are you so angry?"

"Calm down? Calm down!" The spirit voices shriek the words together, over and over until they reach a deafening crescendo.

"Please," Angela shouts through the echoing din. "I'm so sorry. Please... just..." An anguished sob cuts off her words, and she doubles over holding her stomach. Daniel wraps his arm around her shoulders, but she straightens and shrugs him away. "I. Am. So sorry," she manages to say with a quavering voice. "I... I never... meant..."

The spirit voices stop, leaving my ears ringing in the silent corridor. Logan and I exchange a glance. They seem to be gone for now. I don't know whether it's good or bad. They could be off conspiring against us. We continue down the narrow hall, broken glass from multiple shattered pictures crackling beneath our feet. So many torn, ruined faces smiling up at us from the floor. Group sorority photos from every year must have lined these walls. From the devastation, it looks like the spirits were extra vengeful in here. Perhaps year after year of happy faces weighed a bit too heavily on them.

The kitchen isn't much better, but at least the table and several chairs are upright. Broken dishes and glassware litter the floor to the point that the ceramic tile is mostly hidden by the debris. Such immense rage and power. My pulse leaps. Biting my lip, I force my breathing into an even pace. Can't let the ghosts know I'm scared. Paranormal Investigations 101. Everything preys on weakness, from werewolves to vampires to demonic spirits.

"When will they return?" Angela asks as Daniel helps her into one of the sturdy, wooden chairs.

"Don't know." Logan leans against the wall. He crosses his arms over his chest. "We'll just have to wait. Perhaps you should try talking to them, since it's quiet."

"Um, okay." Angela clears her throat. "I came to say I'm sorry. I didn't know… no that's not quite true." She pauses and stares at her hands folded in her lap. "I didn't know the atrocities he planned. I didn't know he'd hurt you. He seemed so nice, so loving. I know now that it was all an act, an act I should have seen through—" She gasps in several quick breaths. "I should have read him. I should have known better. Why did I believe him…" She trails off, burying her face in her hands.

This is deteriorating fast. Logan pushes away from the wall and limps over to Angela. "Tell them your side of the story, Angela. About your relationship and what happened after the… tragedy." He leans down and whispers, "Be strong for them. They've already suffered so much. You can do this."

"O-okay. I remember the day we met as though it were yesterday. He was so charming and so hand-some—every girl in the class couldn't stop staring." She raises her head, staring off at the wall, her eyes glazed. "I will never forget the thrill when he chose me to help him with his research. Me. Of all the girls, he chose me."

When she doesn't continue, Daniel asks, "What kind of research?"

"Oh, it was fascinating. He was doing research for the CIA into mind control and interrogation aids. Jeffrey was so committed to his work."

"I'll just bet he was," Daniel murmurs. I send him a dark glare, and he has the decency to look sheepish.

"Please, Angela, do continue your pathetic love story," a thready, female voice says.

16
Memories & Forgiveness
~

LOGAN

I push back from Angela, ready for battle. But the three spirits float calmly in the center of the kitchen. When a hand grips my arm, I can't help but jump a bit. Kacie whispers an apology as she joins me, blocking Angela from the three ghosts. They don't attack or speak, just continue to hover.

"It didn't seem pathetic at the time," Angela says, peeking around my side to peer at the spirits of her long gone friends. "I was young and in love."

"You were weak and stupid," the three say as one.

Creepy with a capital 'C'. They can obviously communicate telepathically. That can't be good for us.

"I know you're upset, and I can't claim to have even the slightest understanding of the horror you endured,"

Kacie says, stepping toward the filmy phantoms. "You were hurt in a horrible way, went through so much pain and suffering."

"What could you possibly know of our suffering?" One of the spirits separates from the group and towers over Kacie, her form fading from silver to a darker gray. Not good.

"It's me you're angry at," Angela says, reaching out a shaking hand toward them. "Don't take out your anger on her. She's just trying to help."

The spirit moves to tower over Angela. When she doesn't flinch under the spirit's intangible pressure, my respect for her rises a notch. She raises her chin, staring at the angry energy with a calm expression.

"I was there…" Angela's voice hitches and she takes a deep breath. "It was my fault. I can never really tell you how sorry I am. I loved him. I trusted him… and I thought he loved me too."

"How dare—"

Angela cuts the spirit off midsentence. "No, Tracy, please just listen. I have suffered every single day. In and out of institutions, watching the people around me find love, have children, while I couldn't recover from the bitter betrayal. Jeffrey made himself my world. In hindsight I know he used his mind control experiments to mold me into the perfect accomplice, but at the time, I thought it was passion and undying love. When he… when he used me to… well…"

A dark gray spirit appears beside Angela. "Well, come on. You can say it."

Angela's head whips around to look at the new spirit. "Renee! I—I never wanted—"

"Wanted what, Angela?" Renee draws out Angela's name in a mocking tone. "Watch Tracy get hacked to bits? Watch Amy gouge her own cheeks in her terror? But lucky you didn't get to see me destroyed by two cars. You know I lived for a while after. Felt every broken bone, every gash torn in my skin."

"I watched," a third spirit says as she materializes on Angela's other side. For some reason she is still silvery, like the anger hasn't consumed her as much as the others. "I died somewhere on the way down the stairs. While my spirit hovered over my dead body, I saw Renee run by. I called to her, but she didn't hear me, so I chased after her. I don't think I knew I was dead at the time. All I remember is screaming at her to stop. I watched her run toward the street, saw the cars coming from opposite directions. It was so late at night. Why were there two cars out there? It was almost like fate or something. I remember screeching and banging and screaming... then nothing."

Angela chokes back a sob. "Oh, Amy, I can still see everything like a bright-colored movie in my mind. I thought I was having a bad trip. Jeffrey told me not to move because I might hurt myself. I believed him. We'd been studying the effects of LSD, so I assumed... the idea that it was really happening... seemed impossible, even in my haze. But even then, I couldn't just sit by and watch. Jeffrey... he... he tied me up. I tried to fight, but he was so strong."

"I don't blame you," Amy's wavering spirit says. "You were a victim just like us."

"How can you say that?" Tracy says as her spirit energy darkens. "She brought him here. She did nothing to stop him. She knew he was giving us drugs and didn't care!"

"I have to let go of the hate." Amy's silvery visage dims a bit. "Look at her. She's suffered her whole life."

"At least she had a life!" Tracy says, moving to cower over Amy.

"It doesn't sound like it was much of one." Amy floats across the room, her form becoming less tangible. "I forgive you, Angela. Try to forgive yourself... Oh my... the light—it's so pretty, so warm." Her spirit energy floats upwards before fading to nothing.

One down, two to go...

Angela lifts her hand as though to wave, then lowers it. "Goodbye, Amy. Please rest in peace."

"Pathetic."

"Sheesh, Amy always was a softie."

I don't know who said what, but it's obvious these two won't move on quite as peacefully as Amy did. A wave of intense energy batters against the shield formed by my aura merged with Kacie's—a penetrating heaviness that makes my teeth ache. I'd hate to feel that without a psychic shield.

"Again... how? How do you keep us out?" Tracy asks, her ghostly eyes filled with curiosity rather than anger.

I decide to indulge her curiosity... I'll take that over rage any day. "Kacie and I are psychically linked. We can merge our auras and form a barrier of sorts."

Tracy stares at me for a moment, then a large, feral grin spreads across her face, making her look like an evil Cheshire Cat. "Psychically linked... psychically linked." She taps a finger on her chin. "I bet you have no idea just how devastating that will end up being."

"What's so damn funny?" Renee asks as her spirit darkens further. Not good...

"Think about it. What have we learned about psychic energy?"

Tracy giggles, a sound that belongs in a psych ward rather than a sorority house—then again, maybe not. Her hysterical laughter echoes around us, deafening, mocking. When Renee joins in, I have to keep myself from covering my ears. I won't let them know how much they bother me.

"Are you going to share your maniacal thoughts or just laugh?" Kacie snaps, her jaw clenched, but her expression bland.

Tracy stops laughing as though someone threw a switch. "You really don't get it, do you?"

Renee continues to giggle, covering her mouth with an ethereal hand. Interesting... the more they laugh the lighter their spirits become. Both are now the color of mild storm clouds rather than those that create down-pours.

"Enlighten us." My voice is controlled, but my glare is not.

"Ooh, look at the scary, angry boy," Renee says before bursting into more giggles.

"You two are psychically connected." Tracy waves her hand in dismissal, like her words explain everything. I hate feeling slow, but I don't get where they're leading me.

Renee's laughter cuts in an instant. "Love is destined to fail, to die. It never lasts. You two will hate each other someday—probably sooner rather than later."

Tracy's smile turns nasty. "When you can no longer stand the mere thought of the other, you'll still be psychically connected."

"Love is fleeting, but psychic powers are forever." Renee finishes with a big flourish of her arms.

"We aren't in love." The moment the words leave my mouth, I regret them. What if Kacie feels something more than... whatever this closeness and attraction is.

Kacie shakes her head. She looks thoughtful, her eyes far away. Her nose scrunches up the way it does when she's working on a puzzle.

"I really like Logan. But..." She pauses, glancing at me. I nod for her to continue. "But... at this point it's irrelevant anyway. What you're talking about may or may not happen. If we must be psychically connected forever, then we'll have to find a way to deal with it. I can't imagine ever hating him."

"Stupid, naïve girl," Tracy says after a snort of laughter.

"Meh, you're just pissed that your attempt at deflection failed to work," Daniel says, smirking at the pair. "We're here to help you move on or banish you to whatever hell evil spirits go to. One or the other. The choice is yours. But I'm getting bored, and I have a date tonight so let's get this moving."

Another wave of shadowy energy washes over us, leaving the air crackling in its wake. Daniel may be my best friend, but sometimes he can be a bit tactless when dealing with the distraught—people or spirits. Before I can try to smooth things over, the spirit energy darkens along with my vision, dragging me into the depths of their combined memories.

Handsome. Angela is so lucky. I wonder if she'll share. Whatever this new drug is, it's making me feel... free. Free of inhibitions, of worry, of self. My mind floats on a cloud as I watch the professor cuddle up to Angela. He's so hot... yet his eyes are cold. A shiver courses through me when his eyes meet mine. Death. I see death in them. Though I try, I'm unable to break eye contact. Please... I struggle to tear my gaze from his as a horrible sense of foreboding washes over me.

Is it the drugs? Maybe a bad trip? I watch detached as the gorgeous professor's face morphs into something darker... evil. After rummaging through his duffel bag, he pulls out a small bundle, unrolling it with a flourish. Knives. Lots of knives—all different kinds. He pulls out a hunting knife with a curved, ser-

rated edge. My body freezes as he runs the blade down Amy's arm in a quick motion. It's so sharp; I don't think she felt the pain. Maybe he didn't really… no, a deep line of crimson forms on her arm, and she lets out a whimper when she sees the blood.

"Now for a little hide and seek," the nutty professor says as he wipes the knife on a white rag. The blood stains look so stark against the sea of white. I can't take my eyes from it. "I'll count to twenty. Hide or I'll kill you. Now!"

Amy jumps to her feet, an earsplitting scream pouring from her lips. She races from the room while I lurch and stumble to my feet. My head whips from side to side as I try to think of a good place to hide. I run into the hall, colliding with Amy. My head spins. Before I can recover, the professor strolls from the room, slicing arcs through the air with his hunting knife.

"Too slow!" The professor grabs Amy's arm and swipes the knife down her other arm, giving her matching red stripes.

She wrenches away and falls to the floor, trying to scramble away but slipping on the blood that dripped to the hardwood floor.

"Your turn, little girl." He turns to me with a psychotic gleam in his eyes. He drops the hunting knife and pulls a long butcher knife from sheath on his belt. "Better to stab you with."

His maniacal laughter fills the hallway as he lunges for me. I scamper backward but trip over Amy, falling across her prone form. The knife plunges into my thigh. Odd, no pain. All I feel is immense pressure.

"Come on," Amy shrieks as she pulls me to my feet. "Run!"

"Yes, yes, run, little mice. I do enjoy the chase."

Amy drops my hand and races away toward the stairs and potential freedom. I reach the spiral staircase just in time to watch her tumble down, her body crashing on each wooden stair. Screams and loud cracking fill the air around me. Then silence. I lean over the rail to see her body lying in a pool of blood. A broken, discarded ragdoll. My mouth opens to scream. Nothing but a quiet, sobbing mewl emerges.

I wrench myself from the vision, trying to force my focus back to the present while not letting the spirits know they got to me. It's a losing battle. Sometime during the vision, I collapsed. Now I'm lying on the floor, my head resting on Kacie's lap. Our psychic shield is still in place, but beads of sweat have formed on Kacie's forehead from the stress of maintaining it. I feel a firm pressure on my chest, like I dropped the weight bar on myself while doing bench presses. The shadows are larger, looming. I don't think we can hold the shield much longer. It's time for some drastic measures.

"Are you okay?" Kacie whispers in my ear, her voice shaky, revealing her fear.

"Yeah, but I need to go back." Even as the words leave my mouth I realize how crazy they sound. I push up from the floor. For some reason I feel more in control standing. Stupid, I know. I'll probably just collapse again during the vision. But right now... right now I feel the need to appear strong.

"You can't." Kacie grips my shoulder, her fingers digging in. "They're too powerful. You might get... lost."

Lost. Caught between worlds, realms, planes, whatever. A fate worse than death. Entering a vision is similar to astral projection in that the mind separates from the body for a brief time—perhaps merging with the energy of the spirit? It's an unknown. If my mind is torn from my body a coma would result. My body would be whole minus what makes it me. Craptastic.

"No choice," I say, steeling my shoulders. "I have to know what happened to Renee. Her emotions were wild, but I felt guilt. I think that may be what holds her here. She needs to let go of the guilt."

"This is a bad idea," Daniel says, his eyes never leaving the dark shadows looming. "If you have to go, then go... but hurry back." He steps between me and the ghosts, as though that could make any difference if they decide to attack.

"I won't be long." Closing my eyes, I send my psychic power out toward Renee's dark energy. It's like an anti-beacon, and my light zeroes in on the darkness. Electricity thrums in the air, raising the hair on the back of my arms. With a jolt I return to the vision.

I start down the stairs, one timid step at a time, my eyes never leaving Amy's unmoving form. Her neck is bent at an odd angle, her eyes wide and unblinking. Dead. Gone. I back up a couple steps but am stopped by the most anguished wail I've ever heard. Deep, keening, such awful torment. Broken words follow the scream, prayers to God for help. My hand clenches the handrail to the point of pain, my fingernails digging into the cold wood.

Another agonized scream reverberates around me, and I take off running. Ignoring Angela's desperate cries for help, I race down the stairs, tripping over Amy's sprawled legs. I scramble back to my feet and run from the house, horrible screams chasing me like a wailing banshee. My heart pounds to the point of pain, my breath coming in ragged pants. Bare feet slapping the cold pavement, I race away.

Bright lights blind me, and I realize a moment too late that they are headlights. Brakes screech, such an awful sound combined with my own screams. White-hot pain sears through my body as I hit the pavement and skid. Shouting fills my ears, but it's strange—like they're moving farther away the closer they get. Sound fades away leaving nothing but a hollow ringing in its wake. People gather around me, all staring, unmoving. Why aren't they helping me? So tired. I close my eyes and pray for the pain to stop.

Moments later the horrible pain disappears, and I feel light, like I could float away. I open my eyes to find myself floating above the people clustered around my battered body. A beautiful light appears, rainbow, warm and welcoming. I'm drawn toward the light. Peace lies beyond, I'm sure. I drift forward until a terrible scream cuts through my reverie. Angela and Tracy, they're still suffering—I have to help. When I pull away from the light, I feel a rough tearing sensation, like ripping a bandage from a raw, weeping wound.

I abandoned my friends once; I won't do it again...

17

Retreat

~

KACIE

Logan sinks the ground, his knee bending at an awkward angle. Daniel and I each take one of his arms, helping him into a more comfortable position. I kneel beside him, wrapping my arms around his shoulders to lend my strength. Allowing a partial possession is not only draining, it can be downright dangerous. He groans before rubbing a hand across his forehead. The psychic shield we had managed to form is tenuous at best as Logan's blue aura pulses and fades. We're running out of time.

Logan coughs and leans back against me. "I know now. I understand."

"Shh, rest for a minute."

Logan struggles when I try to lean him further back. Instead he leans forward. "Renee, you did nothing wrong."

"I-I don't know—"

Renee is cut off by her livid friend. "You may *think* you know something, but you know nothing of our suffering!" Her words are punctuated by blasts of icy air, leaving us all shivering.

"You're r-right." Logan pushes to his feet. Though he staggers a bit from his injured knee, he waves me away when I try to help him. "There's no way I could understand what you went through that night. But I do understand what Renee is feeling right now because I've been there."

Renee floats toward Logan. "What?" Her voice is soft, curious.

Tracy laughs, a hard, grating mocking of genuine laughter. "You're eating this crap up like a hot fudge sundae."

"It's not crap, Renee," Logan says. He closes his eyes for a few moments as though lost in thought. His nostrils flare, leaving me to wonder what horrors he's remembering. When he opens his eyes, I see nothing but raw determination. Any trace of pain is gone. "I know what you went through, what it's like to want to help in your mind, yet your body won't cooperate."

Renee gasps. "You do know."

"Yes." Logan takes a couple steps forward. "I also know that there was nothing you could have done.

145

Running outside was the best way to get help. If you'd run back to Tracy, *he* would have killed you instead of the cars, but either way you'd still be dead."

"He's lying!" Tracy's form morphs, becoming darker, distorted. "You left me to die with that monster. You ran away."

"I'm sorry, I-I was so scared. My body took control of me, and I ran." Renee backs away from Tracy.

"She refused to go into the light when it appeared for her." Logan's voice is calm and soothing. "Tracy, she stayed for you. Instead of going into the light, she went back to the house. For you."

"No, she abandoned me—"

Logan cuts Tracy off. "No, she didn't."

He glances at me before patting my hand and unwinding my arm from his. His eyes are haunted, from the vision or an awful memory, I'm not sure. When I open my mouth to ask, he shakes his head. He's right, now isn't the time.

"Angela?" Renee calls her in a hesitant voice.

"I'm here, Renee." Angela steps forward until she's only inches from the looming spirits.

Renee's ethereal form morphs again, becoming lighter and more human. "I never really blamed you. You were a victim too."

"I brought—"

"I know, but it's okay. He used you in the worst way possible." Renee reaches out a vaporous limb. "Try to forgive yourself. You don't deserve the pain you've suffered."

Tears fill Angela's eyes and several spill over to run down her cheeks. "Still, I'm sorry. I think about you every single day. Please move on and find peace."

"I will." Her wispy hand appears to caress Angela's cheek then fades away to nothing.

"Is she…" I trail off, my eyes scanning the room. The air is still, as though waiting for something… but what?

"Gone?" Tracy's voice cuts through silence. "Yeah, she's *gone*. Abandoned me again!"

Her frustrated screams echo around us, vibrating the air and sending a blender crashing to the floor. I stare at the shattered pieces while trying to calm my racing heart. A rank stench fills the air, like rotten eggs… perhaps sulfur. It fills my nostrils, burning them. My eyes water. The floor shakes, and I lose my footing, falling against Logan. He stumbles, catching me despite his injured knee. When I glance back to make sure Daniel and Angela are okay, I'm not surprised to see them inching backward away from the maniacal shrieking.

"Tortured, murdered, flayed, broken!" Her volume increases with each shouted word. "Then to return, only to be abandoned by the only, the *only,* two people who knew what I went through—what we went through."

Logan steps forward, pushing me behind him. "We can talk—"

"Talk?"

The dark gray form morphs again until it barely resembles the form of a person. Her spirit grows until it creeps along the ceiling to tower over us. As long, tenuous tendrils reach down, we scuttle backward out of the way.

"While I suffered in life and death, *Angela* got to have a life to live. She caused this and didn't suffer at all."

"But I did suffer—"

"Shut your mouth, you filthy bitch!" Tracy darts over to loom over Angela. "You watched that sadistic bastard kill me and did nothing." She pauses as her form turns inky black. "I will not rest until..." Her words turn into angry, incomprehensible screeching.

Logan grabs my hand. "We need to get out of here... regroup."

Without another word, we race from the house. As we spill out, Angela trips on the striped tent, falling to the ground. Blake appears and hauls her body up and out of the way. His sudden movements still shock me at times, and of course this is one of them. I pause in the doorway, only to be thrown forward when it slams closed. After stumbling a few times, I regain my footing and follow the others away from that cursed house.

~

Angela trudges from the car to her door, her shoulders slumped and her steps slow. The twin cats *meow* together, sorrowful, as they watch her retreating form. Daniel kisses her cheek before closing the door and heading back to the car. My eyes burn, and I bite my lip to keep the tears at bay. She thinks she failed because we couldn't cross Tracy. No matter what anyone said about how we saved Amy and Renee, Angela only focused on her failure. Perhaps that's why she never recovered from the madness forty years ago... because she couldn't see past the negative to anything positive.

To make matters worse, Samson and Delilah have chosen Logan as their new master. Poor Angela doesn't even have the comfort of her familiars.

When Logan takes my hand and curls his fingers around mine, I allow a few silent tears to fall. Four lives were lost that night, not three. Everyone forgets the victim who lived, who suffered years of tormented memories made worse by—

"That's it!" My exclamation rings through the silence in the car.

Rebecca glances at me over her shoulder from the front seat. "Huh?"

"Tracy thinks that Angela didn't suffer, that she can't understand. We need to make Tracy see what Angela's been through."

Daniel sighs. "Angela is broken, Cici. We can't involve her anymore."

Logan glances at me, raw pain in his eyes. "I took her pets…"

"They're familiars… they decide where to go." I squeeze his hand, but the sadness remains.

"She told me she loves dogs and has always wanted one," Daniel says. "Let's get her a dog."

Rebecca snorts. "You can't just get a pet for someone."

"Of course you can." Daniel taps a beat on the steering wheel. "A goldendoodle like Kodiak would be perfect."

"What do you two think?" Logan asks the cats swirling around our ankles. They *meow* in unison, a cheerful, bright sound. "I think they agree." He turns to me with a hopeful look. "Can you find a goldendoodle? Not a puppy, but an older dog?"

I think about my goldendoodle, Kodiak, and have to admit that a dog like that would be great for Angela. "I'll do my best. There are lots of rescues… surely someone has a golden or labradoodle in need of a good home."

Daniel pulls to a stop at my house. As I open the door to get out, Samson and Delilah try to follow me.

Logan gathers the two in his arms. "This isn't our stop yet."

They mewl and settle down, watching me with wide, unblinking eyes. "I'll have Dad or Gavin drop me at your house later for the meeting."

Logan nods. "Six o'clock. I'll order pizza. Pepperoni and peppers?"

"You know what I like." I lean in and give him a quick kiss goodbye. "I'm in the mood for jalapenos tonight."

"Spicy. I like it," Logan murmurs against my lips.

Daniel makes a shooing motion at me, and I back away from the car. "See ya in a few."

I watch them drive away while my crows circle overhead. Before the neighbors can notice the odd gathering above me, I race into the house.

18

Premonition

~

LOGAN

Laughter shakes my body making me wince from the pain searing through my side. With a click of the remote, I turn off the TV. No more comedies until I'm healed.

Mom wrings her hands while darting between tidying the family room and plumping the pillows behind my back. She sucks in a breath before racing to the kitchen. When she returns, she has my tarot deck in her shaking hands.

"Premonition." Her voice is as shaky as her hands as she places the deck on my lap. "A reading. Now."

"Mom, I—"

"Don't argue. Do a reading. Now."

I shuffle the worn deck, once, twice, three times. "How many cards?"

"Just three. Hurry."

The first card I turn over is the Five of Swords. Not surprising at all. "Defeat." Not a great card, but given the events of the day it's appropriate. My hand trembles over the next card. I know what it is without turning it, but I flip it over anyway. The Tower. Trials, tribulations, and turmoil. Craptastic. Without waiting, I flip over the third card. Nine of Swords. "Anguish." There are few tarot readings that I can't but a hopeful spin on... but with these three cards together, I just can't see it. I glance up at Mom, my heart racing at the fear reflected in her eyes.

"What happens if a ghost kills someone?"

Before the Foxblood Demon, before the power I witnessed today, I'd have said it was impossible. But now... "I don't know. Why do you ask?" The tremor in my voice gives away the unease I'm trying to hide. *What isn't she telling me?*

She doesn't answer. Instead she whips out her cell phone. "Roger? It's Marianne. I had a premonition... a bad one." Silence stretches out as she listens to him speak. "Yes, get everyone here as soon as possible. We need to do something before midnight." More silence. "Pour a rim of salt around the pool where the spirit board rests. Remember that blackberry wreath I gave Anna for Christmas last year? Float that on the pool. It will help keep the spirit from accessing any power from the board."

"What's going on, Mom?" Blackberry, salt, none of this sounds good. Both are used to suppress negative spirit activity. "Why did you call Mr. Kincaid?"

"Sweetie, it's so hard for me to explain…" She trails off as she plumps my pillows again, betraying her frayed nerves. "I only want to explain once. Plus I need some time to commune with the Goddess. I want to be sure…"

"Mom…" I call out, but my voice is weak. Samson and Delilah settle at my sides, loud purrs vibrating their lithe bodies. I run my hands down both of their backs, the action soothing my nerves. As my eyes flutter closed, I realize Mom got me again. Sedative in the hot chocolate. I should know better by now…

~

The soft hum of multiple voices awakens me. I stretch my arms over my head before I remember the torn intercostal muscle in my side. Whatever Mom put in the hot chocolate helped with the pain as well. It's nice having a mom who is an expert herbalist. The cats mewl, then stretch their backs and knead their front paws against my legs. Their claws scrape along my jeans, light enough to leave no mark. The spicy scent of marinara and pepperoni wafts across my nose, making my stomach rumble in response. Pizza.

Kacie leans down, her bright smile bringing a returning one of my own. "I brought you two slices, both pepperoni and jalapeno." She sets the paper plate on my lap, and the cats sniff the crust.

"Mine." They look at me with narrowed eyes, displeased with my words.

"Come on, kitties," Kacie says in a cooing voice. "I got you some food on the way over. Fancy Feast… though I really doubt it's all that fancy… still I'm sure you'll like it better than pizza." She heads to the kitchen, my new familiars winding around her ankles.

"Hours of footage and nothing!" Carl's angry voice makes me cringe as he plops down on the sofa beside me.

Do I dare ask?

He glares at me. "Aren't you even gonna ask? Whatever, it doesn't matter. All I have are major EMF spikes and the chair flying through the window. Oh, and of course lots of interviews with overdramatic girls."

"It's not so bad, Carl." Rebecca's voice is soft, like she's trying to calm a scared puppy.

"*Hmph.* Easy for you to say." Carl folds his arms over his chest. "You didn't just spend hours going through useless footage!"

Rebecca waves a slice of pizza under his nose. "C'mon, Carly, you need to eat something."

Did she just call him Carly?

He pushes her hand away. "I'm not hungry."

"Quit pouting and eat already." She shoves the pizza against his mouth, but he refuses to open it. "Look, Logan's eating and he got his ass handed to him again today. You don't see him complaining."

"Back. Off." The words come out harsher than I intended.

Kacie sits on the arm of the sofa beside me. "You okay?" She runs her hand through my hair, brushing her thumb across my forehead.

I close my eyes, letting my head fall back against the sofa. "Is it just me, or did those ghosts seem more focused on me than anyone else."

"Kacie mentioned that." Rebecca sets her plate on Carl's lap and digs through her messenger bag. "I found a picture of the nutty professor. Other than hair color, you two look a bit alike."

I glance at the grainy newspaper photo. "I don't see it."

"I do," Kacie says as she glances between the photo and me several times. "It's in the facial structure."

Rebecca nods. "Yep. It would almost be a subconscious recognition. Our brains are hardwired to recognize faces through structure, even though we don't consciously realize it."

Craptastic.

"We might be able to use that." Rebecca stares at the ceiling as she says the words.

"The least you can do is look at me if you're going to use me as cannon fodder."

Kacie lets out a noise that sounds like a growl. "Hasn't he been through enough?" When Rebecca ignores her, Kacie grabs her arm. "Look at him!"

Her eyes fill with remorse when she glances at me. "I'm sorry, Logan."

"It's okay. I was thinking the same thing anyway."

Kacie wraps her arm around my shoulders. "You've been hit in the head a few too many times."

"That last bookend hurt." I rub the back of my head where the flying menace struck.

"Logan, there's dried blood," Kacie says as she moves my hair aside with gentle fingers. "How hard were you hit?"

"I saw stars." I laugh and she gives me a hard glare. "Tunnel vision for a second or so on the way out."

She lets my hair fall back to cover the evidence. "Why didn't you say anything?"

"Uh... we were running from a pissed off, crazy-ass ghost. Remember."

"Eat something."

"I am."

"You haven't touched your pizza," Kacie says, pointing at my full plate. "Grilled cheese?"

I nod, and she takes the plate from my hands. My stomach couldn't handle the spicy pizza. If I'm going to be any use tonight, I need to fuel up on something that won't make me feel worse. Mom swoops in, taking the plate and rescuing Kacie from cooking. I don't miss the relieved look in my girlfriend's eyes.

"Move over." She taps Carl's leg with the tip of her boot.

"Where's your food," I ask, noticing her empty hands.

"Already ate it." She laughs at my surprised expression. "What? I was hungry. I scarfed it in the kitchen."

"Whoa!" Blake's loud voice booms through the room.

Poe flaps around near the ceiling, circling the room a few times before landing on Kacie's lap.

I glare at Blake. He shrugs. "Sorry. He flew right past me when I opened the door."

Samson and Delilah choose this moment to return from the kitchen. I cringe as they jump up on my lap, waiting for the fur and feathers to fly. Both cats regard Poe who bobs his head a few times and lets out a soft, *caw. Meow,* the cats respond together before settling down on my lap.

"That went better than expected," my mom says, echoing my thoughts. She hands me a plate with a steaming grilled cheese on it. "Blake, honey, grab your dinner so we can all sit down and plan our attack tonight. Oh, and Poe, I left the kitchen window open. Please do your business outside."

Caw. Poe answers, ruffling his feathers.

"Total weirdness," Carl says in his squeaky, I'm-completely-creeped-out-now voice.

"Carl, can it," Rebecca says, punching him in the arm.

"I just call 'em as I see 'em."

"Yeah, well maybe you should close your eyes for a while."

"Enough!"

All eyes focus on Mr. Kincaid who just entered the room.

"Sorry." He pulls off his glasses and rubs the bridge of his nose. "Let's get down to business. Marianne?"

"Earlier I had a premonition, foggy, yet I knew it was bad." She pauses and glances at me. "It felt dire, but I couldn't grasp what the premonition wanted me to know, so I had Logan do a tarot reading."

When she doesn't continue, Mr. Kincaid asks, "Did that help?"

"I think so. Logan, can you summarize the reading?"

Blake interrupts. "Wait a sec. Where's Raven?"

"In my workshop making blackberry wreaths and some herbal pouches for tonight," Mom says, pointing absently down the hall. When Blake rises to search her out, Mom adds, "I don't think she's eaten, take some extra pizza."

"You sure you don't need me?" Though Blake asks, it's obvious he's already decided to go to Raven.

"No, dear, you're muscle tonight."

Blake nods before disappearing down the hall carting two plates filled with pizza. My worn tarot deck lies on the table beside me, watching… waiting. I pick it up and shuffle the cards a few times. The practiced motion eases my tension.

"The cards before were Five of Swords, the Tower, and Nine of Swords," I murmur more to myself than anyone else.

"Oh." Kacie gasps. "I know the Tower is really bad." She grasps my arm. "The last time he did a reading for me, I got the Tower. He doubled my training with Blake. I swear the extra training is what'll kill me."

Snorts of laughter follow her remarks. We've all been on the receiving end of Blake's training. He takes it seriously, like a werewolf should. If he ever leads his pack, anyone can challenge him in a fight for leadership. The fights aren't supposed to be to the death, but they can be deadly nonetheless. Sometimes Blake forgets that we aren't all werewolves fighting for pack position. But for all of Kacie's complaints about the rigid training, she loves it. Occupational hazards are par for the course for the Orion Circle. Be prepared isn't just for Boy Scouts.

"Upright, the card isn't as dire for most people..." I trail off before glancing at Kacie. "For us and our *job* it just isn't true. For us the Tower means a large obstacle that must be overcome. Obstacles in the supernatural world tend to be very dangerous."

"What about the swords," Rebecca asks, her fingers poised to type on her laptop.

"Swords are somewhat bad all around... they stand for strife and turbulence in life. Bad times needed to be overcome. Five of Swords basically stands for defeat—like what we experienced today."

"We moved two people on," Daniel says as he enters the room. "How is that *defeat*?"

"I'm not saying that wasn't good," I say before sighing. "We left behind trouble bigger than those two spirits combined. I did this reading for Mom and her premonition. Defeat represents Tracy's spirit."

"And the Nine?" Rebecca prompts.

"Anguish. Despair. Loss."

19

Danger

~

KACIE

A shudder courses through me—not from Logan's words but the anguish in his voice as he spoke them. I cuddle up against his side, nudging Samson… or is it Delilah? I can't tell them apart yet. The cat stares at me with inscrutable eyes before moving and curling up on my other side. As I lean up against Logan's side, Poe hops from my leg to my hip. He walks around a few times then settles down on top of the purring cat. Damn, I wish I had my cell handy.

"Logan's reading confirmed my premonition," Mrs. Finley says, wringing her hands together. "I saw shadows enter the sorority house, heard screams, saw death."

Rebecca tips her head. "Death?"

"Yes. The Grim Reaper... the embodiment of death. I think the nine swords represent some overly curious individuals who plan to sneak into the house tonight."

Carl leaps to his feet, knocking Rebecca's laptop to the floor. "*Nine* people are going to sneak in there and ruin everything I set up? Uh, not to mention get themselves killed!"

"Damn it, Carl, chill." Rebecca leans down and snatches her laptop from the plush carpet. "You're being too literal again. How many times have I told you —"

"Carl, sweetie, sit down." Mrs. Finley's soothing voice calms Carl enough that he sinks back down to the sofa. "It really doesn't matter if it's one or one hundred people sneaking in. What I foresaw was bad."

"We need to get down there and neutralize this ghost before anyone has a chance to trespass," Rebecca says.

Mr. Kincaid nods. "Agreed. That leads us to the how. After everything that's happened, I can't allow anyone else to enter that house without a definitive plan."

"What are our options?" Rebecca asks as she gathers her hair into a messy ponytail. "I wasn't there and haven't been briefed."

"We crossed two of the spirits, Renee and Amy." I reach down and run my hand along Poe's soft feathers. The cat at my side butts my hand with its head, begging

163

for attention. "Which cat is this?" I ask Logan in a whisper.

"Samson."

I run my fingers through Samson's silky fur, finding solace in the soothing motion. "Tracy went bat crap crazy. I think Rebecca's theory about shadow people origins may be correct. She was changing, warping right before our eyes."

"It was like every angry outburst darkened her spiritual energy," Daniel says while pacing the floor. "She seemed to be the ringleader, the one who would rile up the other two. When they moved on, it infuriated her. She screamed about being abandoned again."

"Abandonment issues?" Rebecca types on her keyboard. "I haven't really found anything about the three girls online, well not background issues anyway. I didn't try family… wait. Found her. It's an article from 1963 about a car accident. It killed her parents. Don't know what happened to Tracy after that. Maybe shipped around to relatives?"

Mr. Kincaid nods. "That or foster care."

"She was also angry that Angela got to live while she died," Logan adds.

"On that note, I thought of something earlier." I lean back as Poe hops across me, heading toward Logan's plate. He grabs a piece of bread crust in his beak and settles down on my lap.

Carl snorts. "Weird doesn't even begin to describe that."

"Shh," Rebecca admonishes. "Go ahead, Kacie."

"People tend to concentrate on the victims and forget the survivors. Angela had a terrible life after the murders. The trial itself had to be an ordeal. She was in and out of mental hospitals. Maybe if we can make Tracy understand how much Angela has suffered, she might calm down."

Rebecca's fingers click away on the keys. "It says here that she was originally charged as an accessory to murder one. She pled out and agreed to assist the DA. In return for testifying, the accessory charges were dropped to felony mischief. She received a thousand hours of community service."

Logan frowns. "That seems rather harsh, given she was a victim as well."

"You have to understand the culture in the early seventies," Rebecca says. "The whole MKUltra thing was unheard of. Modern behavioral psychology was in its infancy. What the police and the court saw was a girl besotted enough with a man that she'd do anything for his love and his drugs. And this was also on the heels of the Manson murders, which to this day are memorable to say the least. I think they wanted to send a message that this type of excuse would not be tolerated. It never occurred to them that the depraved professor used drugs and emotional abuse to create an almost Stockholm Syndrome with her."

"Stockholm Syndrome?" Carl asks, scrunching up his face. "Isn't that a bit extreme? She wasn't a kidnap victim held prisoner for years."

Rebecca shakes her head. "Maybe not but emotional and physical abuse in a relationship can also lead to Stockholm-like characteristics. She was manipulated emotionally through the use of suggestion and drugs by someone she admired. Over time, she lost all sense of self as she became immersed in his fantasy world."

"Problem is… she didn't stay in that fantasy world." My chest aches, a dull pressure that makes it hard to breathe. I can only imagine what that poor girl felt when she was finally herself again. Despair, hopelessness, self-loathing. "Once separated from him and the drugs, she recovered fairly quickly. Then she couldn't live with what she had done."

"Add to that the trauma of the trial…" Daniel stops his pacing to meet my eyes. "Can you imagine what a circus that must have been? The photos, the statements, all while having to be in the same courtroom with the monster who tormented her."

"You're right on that account," Rebecca says after some rapid typing. "The defense tried to paint Angela as the instigator and murderer. According to accounts, the cross-examination was brutal. I can't find a transcript of the trial… not that I'd want to read it anyway. All I know is that Angela didn't make it through the trial. She suffered a mental breakdown on the stand. The defense didn't go for insanity or anything, even though Dr. Rosenthal was caught at the scene of the crime covered in the blood from all four victims."

Carl looks up. "Four?"

Rebecca nods. "Four. Angela's blood was on him too." She pauses and continues to scan the story on her laptop. "When Angela was led from the sorority house in handcuffs, she was covered in blood—her own blood, but no one knew that yet. The media painted them as Bonnie and Clyde serial murderers for two weeks until the police announced that Angela was cleared of any murder charges. I can't believe the defense tried to pin the whole thing on her." Rebecca lets out a wry laugh. "Stupid plan, didn't work."

"Doesn't matter much though," Logan says. "Angela never recovered from the ordeal."

"She never lived her life," I say, biting my lip. "She never got over what happened, never moved on. She's been living in her own version of Purgatory for forty years."

"No kidding." Rebecca's fingers hit the keyboard in an angry staccato. "Would you believe that crazy professor wrote a book from death row? He was also interviewed by numerous media personalities, and lived life in the limelight until he was executed."

"Perfect for someone with a narcissistic personality," Mrs. Finley murmurs.

"That totally sucks." Daniel resumes his restless pacing. "The freak criminal is immortalized, and the victim suffers as a pariah."

"We need to show Tracy how much Angela suffered," I say, feeling a burst of determination. "She needs to know that her murderer was convicted and executed years ago. Angela has suffered daily and never lived her life. Tracy needs to know that Angela never forgot about her, thought about her every day of her life."

Logan pats my shoulder. "Sounds great in theory. But I think she's far beyond listening."

"I agree," Mr. Kincaid says. "In fact, I'm not sure I can, in good conscience, let any of you back in that house."

"I agree... what did Anna say?" Mrs. Finley asks, referring to Mrs. Kincaid, our Circle chapter leader.

"She arranged for an exorcism team to meet us at the house in an hour." Mr. Kincaid taps at his phone a few times. "Chief Diving Eagle, Pastor Emilio and his assistant Rosalina, along with..." He pauses, his eyes moving to Mrs. Finley. "You, Marianne."

"No, Mom," Logan says, struggling to his feet. Though he groans at the pain, it doesn't stop him from striding up to his mother. "It's far too dangerous."

"Really, honey?" She lets out a nervous laugh. "You still plan to go there tonight, and yet expect me to just allow it."

"But an exorcism? It isn't the same." Logan crosses his arms over his chest, wincing from the movement.

"Do you have any idea how hard it is for your father and me to allow you to dive into these dangerous situations?" Mrs. Finley wraps her arms around his shoulders and leads him back to the sofa. "You have a gift, and so do I. We have a duty to use our gifts to help others. You can't protect me any more than I can protect you, dear."

Logan flops down on the sofa, letting out a pained hiss. When he glances at me with pleading eyes, I shake my head. Nothing I say will change Mrs. Finley's mind either. I place my hand on his thigh, stroking his leg through his jeans.

"There's a simple solution," I murmur, leaning my head close to his. He looks at me with such hope, I feel guilty about my next words. "We move Tracy on… convince her to go into the light on her own. Then no exorcism."

"The Circle didn't use an exorcism last time," Rebecca says. "Will that make a difference over the banishment ritual they used?"

"An exorcism isn't permanent," Mrs. Finley says as she eases herself down into a blue armchair. "Spirits, demonic or otherwise, can return, exorcism or no. It's a more intense form of eviction and may last longer than a simple cleansing or banishment ritual. An exorcism is for powerful spirits, the stubborn ones who are too powerful for their own good."

"And demons," Raven says as she enters the room carrying a bundle of greenish wreaths and small pouches. She places them on the end table beside our high priestess. "We were low on blackberry so I wove in some clove and ivy."

"Good thinking, dear," Mrs. Finley says while inspecting the wreaths. "You have a real talent for herbs."

Raven bows her head. "Thank you, High Priestess."

Blake stands behind Raven, almost as though he's her bodyguard. His dark eyes never leave her, stalking her movements like the wolf he is. Silence continues as Mrs. Finley and Raven pass out the wreaths and pouches. The wreaths go around our necks, and I'm happy there aren't any mirrors nearby. I'd rather not see how ridiculous I look sporting a wreath. Pouches of mixed protection herbs are placed in our pockets. I inhale, enjoying the woodsy aroma. If nothing else, at least we all smell pleasant.

Mrs. Finley sits down beside me. "How is that bracelet working?"

"Fine. But I have to admit… it drives me crazy with the constant vibrating."

"Does it distract you? When you're on a case?"

I think about her words. "No. I'd like to say yes, because I do find it annoying. But the vibrations ebb and flow with the surrounding negative energy. I can sense psychic attacks coming seconds earlier than before. It's becoming more a part of me every day."

"Good, good." She pats my leg. "That's what I hoped to hear."

Logan groans beside me, and we both turn to him. "Premonition," he murmurs in a strained tone while clutching his head with his hands.

"What did you see, dear?" Mrs. Finley asks, her voice calm and soothing.

He drops his hands and leans his head back against the sofa. Samson and Delilah let out simultaneous *mewls* and butt his legs with their heads. He moans again, his fingers clenched in his hair like he might tug it out. Premonitions seem to be painful for him. I don't have them, so I don't understand why.

"It… hurts." A cold sweat breaks out on his forehead, and I motion for Blake. He doesn't hesitate, having seen this before.

Blake's quick reaction eases the tension in my shoulders, and I allow myself to relax a bit. There is something so refreshing about the werewolf. Even as I cradle Logan in my arms, I can't help but be relieved at Blake's quick understanding and action. Everyone in the Circle is always full of questions. Blake too but he is also action-prone—he does what's needed and asks questions later. He returns from the kitchen, handing me a rag soaked in cold water, and I place it on Logan's forehead, wiping in gentle motions. Everyone remains silent as we wait for Logan to recover and reveal what he saw. He takes the rag from my hands, running it across the back of his neck.

"Honey, what did you see?" his mother asks.

"Death."

20

Death Omen

LOGAN

Pain lances through my head, and I bite back another groan. Can't let anyone know how messed up I really am, or they won't let me hunt. After this premonition, I know I have to be there. Everyone stares at me... waiting for the big reveal, but I can't find the words. My stomach drops as I recall the hazy image, the unseeing gray eyes. I just saw my best friend's death.

I run the wet washcloth over the clammy skin at the nape of my neck. A shiver courses through me, traveling from my torso down my arms and legs. I feel detached, floating. Part of me wants to ride that detachment right into insanity. But I force myself back into the present. I can feel again: the soft fur of my familiars beneath my fingers, Kacie's breath against my cheek as she whispers words of encouragement, and

Poe pulling at my hair, tickling my ear with his beak. Really? It's the crow that finally pulls me from the darkness.

"Enough, Poe." I gently prod at the crow until he hops off my shoulder. He lands on the back of the sofa, his beady eyes never leaving me.

"You back?" Kacie asks in a soft voice.

"Yeah… but…" I trail off, unable or maybe unwilling to continue. Premonitions are scary things—twisted, hazy, hard to understand. Yet this one was the clearest I've ever had. Daniel's dead, unseeing eyes staring up at me from his prone body. I didn't see the surroundings. I don't know where or when it will happen. I don't know anything!

"I need everyone to clear out." Kacie makes a waving motion with her arm. "Please, it's important." Everyone stands and heads toward the kitchen in silence. "Wait, Raven, I need your help."

She sits on the chaise by my leg. "What do you want me to do?"

"Take his other hand," Kacie says as she takes my right. "Logan, close your eyes."

I take a deep breath and close my eyes.

"Listen to my voice." Kacie squeezes my hand. "Raven and I are open to you. Use our strength, our psychic power. Visualize your premonition. Is it fuzzy?"

"Yes."

"What do you see?"

"Daniel."

Kacie and Raven both gasp in unison.

"What is Daniel doing?" It's Raven's voice. Kacie must be too shocked to speak yet. It will only get worse. Raven pulls on my hand. "Concentrate! What is Daniel doing?"

"H-he's… dead."

Silence. Complete utter silence.

Raven recovers first. "Are you sure? I-I mean are you sure he's dead?"

My eyes burn through my closed lids. "Yes. No question."

"Where is he?" Kacie asks in a shaky voice. "Can you see where it happened?"

"No. Everything's dark. God, D-Daniel," I say, choking on the words. "Stop. Stop making me see this!"

Raven grips my hand harder, covering it with her other hand. An arm encircles my shoulders, and Kacie leans her head close, resting against my cheek. Her aura pulses, dark red, full of power. Red is never calming. But it fills me with strength and determination, clouding my doubt. The image sharpens, and I can see things I missed before in my grief. A room, in disarray, horrible disarray. Daniel wearing jeans and a gray t-shirt lying in a pile of shattered glass. A large shadow figure looms above him, reaching down with dark, ethereal limbs.

My eyes fly open. "The sorority house," I say through a gasp. "He was killed at the sorority house." I think... it's still too hazy to make out anything but the glass and the dark phantom, but can I take the chance? Hell no.

Raven lets out a relieved sigh. "So if he doesn't go to the house, then he won't die."

I glance at Kacie and see the worry clouding her eyes. She and I both know that it's never that easy.

"I don't like that look you two just exchanged. Spill."

I run my hand through my hair a few times until I'm sure it's sticking straight up from my abuse. "It's a bit more complicated than that..." The image of Daniel's sightless eyes fills my mind, and I trail off, unable to continue.

"Until Tracy is moved on or exorcised, Daniel could be in danger," Kacie says, clutching my hand. "If *she* even is the danger."

"I don't understand. If you saw him dead at the house, then if we keep him away, it won't happen. R-right?" Raven's voice hitches.

"The future is always in motion, even the tiniest change can have vast consequences," I reply, meeting her stricken gaze. "The Butterfly Effect. Heard of it?"

Raven tips her head. "Sort of."

"It's a chaos theory in physics. The smallest thing can have catastrophic effects down the line."

"But you're talking hours or a day or so, not years or centuries."

"Each decision, each action we make affects the future. I'm pretty sure I saw Daniel in the sorority house. But that was a frozen moment in time, continuing down a certain path. We don't know what that path is, what decisions led to his death. If we make different choices, he could still die, only somewhere else."

"It doesn't matter. We could talk about it forever and still never understand a premonition. We need to protect Daniel. Raven, you need to stay here. Put up a protective circle and keep him in it until we take care of Tracy," Kacie says, hugging Samson to her chest. The cat doesn't fight. Instead it relaxes against her, letting out a loud, soothing purr.

"Good idea," I agree.

"Who are you taking instead of Daniel?" Raven asks.

"Mom told Blake earlier that he was muscle tonight. I thought it an odd phrase at the time, but now it makes perfect sense. Let's get everyone back in here. We're running out of time, and between my premonition and Mom's vision, we have lots of lives to save tonight."

~

Even in the darkness, the striped tent looks ominous. Wind gusts, sending a ripple through less secured sections. The back of my neck prickles, and I feel like I'm being watched. I glance around. No curious faces, no movement in the bushes around the house. We seem to be alone. Covered by the tent, the house looks like a carnival attraction, a funhouse, only there's no fun waiting inside.

We watch the house in silence from the relative safety of Blake's pickup. There are only three of us: Kacie, Blake, and me. Everyone else stayed behind after some bitter arguing. Rebecca and Carl would just be potential casualties. We don't need extra cannon fodder… that's my job. They stayed behind at my house to help protect Daniel along with Raven.

Two dark sedans pull up behind us—the exorcism team and Mr. Kincaid. Showtime.

The moment I open the door, Samson and Delilah leap to the ground. My familiars refused to stay behind by attaching themselves to my jeans with their claws. I've always been taught to listen to one's familiar, so their worry was misplaced. I join Blake and Kacie on the sidewalk, and we face the demon house together. Or would that be the demon inside the house?

The air is heavy with negative energy, and for a brief moment I wonder what it would be like to be oblivious like so many other people. I take in a deep breath and almost choke on the thick air. Everything is so quiet. Other than the ambient noise of the nearby freeway, it's as though time has stopped, waiting to see what will happen.

Blake shakes like a dog. "Damn, the air is heavy tonight." He meets my gaze, and I have to fight not to look away. "Something bad…"

Bad. Well, he should be an expert. I shared the worst night of my life with Blake almost five years ago.

What happened… it wasn't his fault, I know that. But every time I look at him I see… *Stop!* I won't make it through tonight if I give Tracy more fodder to use against me. Putting Blake and me together for this was a bad idea. What was Mom thinking?

"The longer we stand out here, the worse it will be," I say, my eyes returning to the tented house. "She's waiting."

Mom runs to my side. "They're here. The ones I foresaw are already inside."

As though on cue, a howling scream rips through the night, shattering the stillness. Anguish and raw fear. Goosebumps follow a shiver that races down my arms.

"We're all going in together," Mr. Kincaid says in a high-pitched tone I've never heard from him before. "There's no time for anything else. Blake, help me rescue the civilians, get them outside."

Blake nods. "You got it."

The Comanche tribal elder steps forward, and Kacie throws her arms around his neck before he can speak.

"Chief Ken, it's so good to see you again!"

Ken? I thought the chief's name was Diving Eagle…

"Little Kassandra?" He holds her out at arms-length. "My dear, you have grown into a beautiful and powerful young woman."

"Thanks to you and your help when I needed it most." She backs away, a blush blossoming across her cheeks.

I'm guessing based on her expression that this is the chief who helped her with her ghost cowboy. I still can't believe she endured a twisted ghost stalker for so long before finding help.

"Friends," the chief says, bowing his head. "The exorcism team is here as a last resort. This spirit has already been banished once, and after speaking with Rebecca, I believe it is not in anyone's best interest to exorcise her. She needs to be moved on, not just for her salvation but to keep this from repeating again in the future."

"She is dangerous and too powerful for her own good," Mom says, her wide eyes never leaving the tented house. "But she is also suffering greatly. Use that suffering to your advantage. Empathize."

My heart pounds so hard I can feel the beat in my throat. Without a word, I slip the blackberry wreath over my head while fingering the herbal pouch in my pocket.

Pastor Emilio clears his throat. "Our main concern is the safety of the people inside and you three." He motions at Kacie, Blake, and me. "If things get out of hand, you'll need to leave so the adults can deal with it."

I can't hide my glare. "I appreciate your concern, Pastor, but we are trained to handle situations like these. This isn't a demon you can send back to Hell. This is a misguided person." This is exactly why I hate it when the adults get involved, especially those without *talent*.

"Now, Logan, we wouldn't be acting responsibly if—"

The chief cuts him off. "You underestimate these teenagers. Their spiritual energy is strong." He turns to us with a grim look. "We will defer to you."

"Ken, that's irrespon—"

"No, it isn't. Spirituality has little to do with age," the chief says, refusing to back down. "I know you are new to Circle affairs, but you must become accustomed to allowing the members to do their duty."

Pastor Emilio rounds on my mother. "How can you serve your son up to potential slaughter?"

Mom closes her eyes, and I know she's praying to the Goddess for strength. "Emilio, I appreciate your concern. I'm concerned as well, but Logan and the Circle members, they're professionals. This is what they do. You must look beyond age to talent. Now while we have argued, Tracy had more time to torture innocents."

Blake strides to the tent flap. "It's time." His voice holds the authority of an alpha werewolf, one who will one day lead his pack. Even the adults are compelled to obey. He disappears through the opening. Taking Kacie's hand, I pull her through with me, assuming the exorcism team will follow.

21

Trespassers

~~

KACIE

As we enter the house, I'm blinded. It's so dark in here, no ambient light—the tent blocks out the moonlight and reflections from nearby streetlamps. Something crashes upstairs, followed by thudding footsteps, then silence again. My bracelet dances on my wrist, and I have to calm my breathing to overcome the innate fear of the dark... of things that go bump in the night. Another loud crash. Lots of things are going bump here tonight. A flashlight flares to life, lighting our immediate vicinity. Debris litters the floor, as though a storm went through destroying everything in its path. I suppose it did—a supernatural storm.

"Thanks." I take the flashlight from Blake, and illuminate him while he pulls another from a small backpack.

More flashlight beams brighten the foyer, as everyone gathers to survey the scene. Gasps, bobbing flashlights, and a softly muttered curse. I take a few steps in, shining my flashlight on the ground so I can avoid the debris. My steps are silent in my hiking boots. Blake joins me, making no attempt at stealth. He kicks and shoves the bigger pieces aside, clearing a path to the door within seconds. Another loud *thud* sounds from upstairs. I shine my light on the staircase, almost dropping it when I see red. The once cream-colored carpet is now crimson on the bottom steps. Gulping, I shine the light further up the stairs. Red continues as far as my beam reaches. My stomach drops. So much blood.

"It's not blood," Blake murmurs. "Mostly anyway. I do smell fresh blood, but not enough to kill someone. More like an injury bleeding."

I shake a bit from relief. "Thank God for your nose. What is it?"

"Tomato sauce or soup or something. How the hell did that get on the stairs?"

I don't bother answering his question. It doesn't matter anyway. Maybe Tracy decided to move from flying objects to painting the house with food.

Or… "Oh, no. Please don't tell me these guys broke in here to add to our pretend prank."

Logan lets out a noise that sounds like a growl. "I think you're right about the prank gone wrong. Maybe we should leave the punks to their fate."

Mr. Kincaid steps forward, shining his light on the red stairs. "Can you tell how many people are here and where they are?"

"Nah, the whole house smells like people." Blake shrugs. "My nose isn't that good. These girls use so much damn perfume." He sniffs again and lets out a light sneeze. "Makes it hard to differentiate smells."

"Noise is coming from upstairs," Logan says, glaring at the staircase like it's the enemy instead of a ghost. "Think everyone's up there?"

"I can carry you if you need it," Blake says as though it's the most normal thing in the world... to offer to carry someone upstairs.

"It's really the down I'm worried about. With my knee as bad as it is..."

Deafening crashes followed by a low moan echoes from further inside, this time downstairs. I thought she'd already destroyed everything—what did she break this time?

"I-I can't..." the pastor's assistant mutters as she inches back toward the door.

"Rosalina, stop." Pastor Emilio's voice is sharp, and she halts the moment he speaks. "You can fall apart later when this is over. Right now we have a job to do."

Mr. Kincaid moves forward, sweeping his flashlight beam around the foyer. "We need to split up." He pauses when another loud crash sounds from somewhere down the hall. "Blake, Kacie, you go upstairs with Ken. The rest of us will check down here." He glances at Blake. "Get the trespassers out to the front lawn. Don't worry about them beyond that. Kacie may need you."

"Um, I volunteer to watch them outside," Rosalina says after a lingering look at the pastor. "I think I'll be more help out there than in here."

The pastor nods. "Good idea. Go on outside and wait."

Rosalina doesn't wait a moment longer. She races to the door almost tripping over the tent flap on the way out. The door swings on its hinges before slamming shut, shuddering in its frame. I cross my arms over my chest waiting for another sign from Tracy. Only silence. My fingers dig into my upper arms. For some reason the silence is more unnerving than the crashes and screams.

"You ready?" Blake asks, placing his hand on my shoulder.

"I hope so."

"I'll go first. Stay close behind me."

"Wait!" Logan grabs Blake's arm. "Take care of *her*." He stares at Blake, his expression far too dark for the situation. And why did he put so much stress on the word her? Seconds tick by as they continue to stare each other. Something's going on between them, and I can't help but wonder if this might explain Logan's aversion to werewolves.

"I promise," Blake says before climbing the stairs.

I put my hand on Logan's forearm. "Stay safe."

After he nods his agreement I creep up the stairs behind Blake. The elder follows behind me. Our footsteps are muted by the carpet, but the house is at least sixty years old and the stairs creak under our weight. I shine my flashlight beam straight at my feet. But when I think about it I almost laugh. We're trying to sneak up on a ghost who probably knew the moment we pulled up in front of the house. She knows were coming. And she's waiting.

We reach the second-story landing, and that's when I realize this house has three stories. Blake pauses, shining his flashlight up the second flight of stairs then down the long dark hallway. Any decision is taken from our hands when we hear a groan coming from further down the hall. Doors hang open on either side of us as we slowly make our way down. At each door, Blake shines his light into the room, doing a quick sweep before closing the door and moving on to the next. About halfway down the hall we reach a door that's closed rather than open. Since the last five were wide open, I have a feeling that we found Tracy's hideout.

Though my bracelet has been dancing nonstop since we pulled up to the curb in front of the house, it starts vibrating so hard it jars my entire arm. I put my hand on Blake's shoulder and point to my bracelet. He nods, and his shoulders stiffen as he prepares himself for what lies beyond the door. My heart hammers. I hate this part of the investigation, of any investigation—the part where I know something lies behind a closed door, and I know it's my job to open the door yet that's the last thing I want to do.

Blake motions at me to open the door for him. He'll go in first, protect us from anything that might attack on entry. I want to tell him he's wasting his time. We're after a ghost, an entity who can blink out and reappear anywhere, anytime. I reach for the knob, enclosing my fingers around the cold metal. Before turning it, I send my aura out, trying to feel the energy of the room. There's just too much negative energy in this house. I can't tell if Tracy lies beyond this door. With one last glance at Blake, I turn the knob and push the door open. It bounces against something inside and swings back.

He shoulders the door open, pushing against the leg of someone lying on the floor. I follow him through the door, sending my flashlight beam out to search the small room. Other than the body on the floor, the room seems empty. Blake kneels on the ground beside the body, a boy, maybe college age, maybe high school. The boy groans as Blake checks his pulse and rolls him over to his back.

"Help," he says in a hoarse voice. "She... she..."

"Shh," Blake says while scanning him for injuries. "Are you hurt? Can you walk?"

"My ankle." The boy sits up with a groan. Now that I can see his face, it's clear that he's young, high school or maybe even middle school. "I-I think... I think it's broken."

"Any other serious injuries?"

"No." The moment he replies, Blake swings him up over his shoulder like he weighs nothing.

"I'll be right back, princess." Blake gives me serious eyes. "Don't leave this room."

I nod. As I wander around the room, my light shines on the normal furniture and things you'd expect to find in a college girl's room. Posters decorate the wall, and I grin when I see Avenged Sevenfold. A girl after my own heart. Though my bracelet still vibrates like a second heartbeat, other than the negative energy there is no sign Tracy. I sit down on the bed covered in a lacy, pink comforter, trying to decide whether I should open myself up to the spirit world. My shields are still up... perhaps it would be wise to wait for Blake to return.

"You should wait for your friend," Chief Ken says as though reading my thoughts. Knowing him maybe he was.

~

LOGAN

In silence we pick our way through the scattered debris littering the floor. It looks like a tornado blew through, damaging the contents while leaving the house standing. How the sorority will explain this to the insurance company, I have no clue. Vandalism maybe? I resist the urge to look over my shoulder to check on my mother. She's perfectly capable of taking care of herself, I know this, and yet the urge to yell at her to get out is strong. Mom still suffers from my sister's death five years ago. With Mom, Blake, and me all in the same house, I'm afraid Tracy will manage to pick up on this and torture her with the heinous death over and over.

Crap, crap, crap! I'm thinking about it. Mom's not the weak link, I am. I fill my head with images of Kacie in Daniel's arms. There. She can think the kiss still bothers me. Unfortunately, the moment I think about Daniel, I remember my premonition. Now all see are Daniel's cloudy, unseeing gray eyes.

"My, my, you're just a mess tonight aren't you?" Tracy appears before me, her spirit reflecting dark gray in my light.

"Tracy." I tip my head, trying to remain calm while hoping she didn't see my thought about Daniel. "You're looking a tad drab tonight."

She laughs, or cackles, yeah a villainous cackle. "Oh, I'm rather enjoying the new me. It's exhilarating."

"You should put more thought in when you're gambling with your eternal soul."

"So serious." She laughs again before morphing her form and looming above me. "But I have other more *interesting* things to do right now."

I control my breathing and keep my face a blank mask. She flickers in and out while swirling around me.

"Nothing? Not even a hitch in your breath... Hopefully your girlfriend will be more fun."

She disappears into the ceiling, and I bite the inside of my cheek to keep from yelling at her to come back. I have to trust Kacie to take care of herself. Hell, she's a more powerful medium than I am… though that could be more trouble than help. My thoughts are wrenched away from her when I hear a grunt coming from somewhere ahead. When I reach the family room, everything appears the same, other than the two guys lying near the broken fireplace. One is unmoving, the other sits up rubbing his head while groaning. As I approach, he sees me and lets out a high-pitched shriek.

"Hey, it's okay. I'm Logan Finley; I'm here to rescue you." If the guy gets my reference to *Star Wars* he chooses to ignore it.

"G-gh-gh-gh—"

"Ghost?" I ask, wondering for a moment if he was channeling Shaggy from *Scooby Doo*.

He nods, then leaps to his feet and races past me into my mother's arms. She hugs him, cooing soft platitudes. I limp to the prone figure, and lower myself to the ground. My knee goes out, and I fall the last foot, banging my ass on the brick pieces littering the floor.

"Son of a—"

"Logan Orpheus Finley!" Mom's voice cuts off my curse. "Language."

Thank God none of my friends are nearby to hear her shout my middle name. I ignore her and place my fingers on his neck.

"Pulse is strong," I call out before placing my hand on his chest. "His breathing seems steady. Should we call EMS?"

Pastor Emilio kneels beside me. "I was a medic in the Army before I got the calling." He examines the body without moving him. "Looks like blunt force trauma to the left temple."

"He got hit with a flying brick," his friend says, looking over his shoulder.

Originally I thought these guys were high school, but now looking at the boy cowering in Mom's arms, I'm thinking middle school.

"He's coming around," Pastor Emilio murmurs. "Shh, there now, son. Are you okay?"

His eyes fly open, and he looks around frantically as he scrambles into a sitting position. Fortunately for him, Tracy is nowhere in sight. I hope Kacie's not having too much of a problem with her.

Mr. Kincaid steps forward. "If you can stand, I'd like to get you and your friend outside."

The boy springs to his feet, making me a tad envious. I guess the spirit wasn't quite as nasty to him as she was to me. Using the broken mantel, I push myself back to my feet. As I dust off my jeans, a gust of icy wind blows by, completing the task for me.

"Aww, you took away my fun," Tracy says, her dark form swirling around me. "Now I guess I'll have to play with you!"

Loud hisses break through the roar of the wind. Samson and Delilah appear beside me, their eyes glowing in the darkness. Together they swipe at the misty spirit with their claws, and she disappears, leaving behind nothing but an echoing laugh.

"Thanks," I murmur to my new familiars.

As I lean down to pet them, their ears prick up in unison. Silence fills the air around us, and though I concentrate, I can't hear anything. But the cats do. Their backs arch and their silky tails fluff up. Before I can try to soothe them, they dart off toward the front of the house. Are they worried about Kacie? Though I want to run—who am I kidding—limp to check on her, I force myself to choose duty over heart. It sucks on so many levels, but I have a job to do.

22
Ghastly Vision

~

KACIE

Heavy footsteps pound on the stairs, and within moments Blake appears in the doorway. "Got him outside. Just hope your ghost doesn't head out there." He glances between the two of us. "Something's going on. What did I miss?"

"She's here… watching… waiting." I send my aura out just a little. But that tiny crack in my shields is just what Tracy was waiting for. Before I can slam my shields back in place, she jumps me trying to take over.

"Kacie!"

I hear Blake's voice calling me. I feel the chief's hands gripping my upper arms. But I feel detached from my body—the first sign of an impending possession. Tracy worms her way into my mind and continues to fight for control. She shrieks before slamming her energy against my shield so hard that it wavers and almost breaks. I hold her at bay. Somehow.

"Stop. Can't help you if you take me over..."

Tracy's voice comes out a hiss like an angry snake. "Who says I want your help. Maybe I just want your body."

"Bigger baddies then you have tried and failed." With a burst of adrenaline-fueled rage I push her out. "If the Foxblood Demon couldn't control me, there's no way some tantrum-throwing sorority ghost will."

Icy wind gusts through the room, picking up papers and creating a small funnel.

"If you were trying to piss her off, I think you succeeded," Blake says, pushing me behind him.

I pat his shoulder. "It's okay." I lower my voice. "I know what I'm doing. Trust me." I take a deep breath. "You want me to understand?" I yell to Tracy through the howling wind. "Show yourself. Talk to me." I open my arms as though beckoning her for a hug. "I'm right here. Come on."

Blake realizes what I'm about to do but too late to stop me. "No!"

"Let her do what she must," the chief says. "While she distracts Tracy we can rescue the other interlopers." He points to the doorway. Another boy and a girl watch the crazy scene with wide eyes. Too scared to run?

When Tracy's powerful energy hits me, I'm knocked backward. But I'm ready for her, and I control my fall to the bed. Her memories flood my mind, and this time I welcome them.

Screaming. Blood. Confusion.

"Please. Please don't do this!" Angela says through wracking sobs.

I watch, detached as my mind floats on a sea of confusion. I should run like Renee and Amy, yet I'm glued to the floor. Jeffrey continues to bind Angela with lengths of rope. She struggles, but he's so strong, no amount of kicking or screaming seems to work. I should have gone home for Thanksgiving. If I'd been gone, I wouldn't be trapped here in my own body watching him run a knife down Angela's arm.

She shrieks again. "I'm sorry. I'm sorry. P-please stop…"

He tears a pillowcase into strips and ties one around her mouth to muffle her endless screams. "Are you going to scream for me, little one?" he asks me as he approaches with the bloodied bowie knife.

My heart thumps so hard that my pulse roars in my ears. I want to scream, to move, but something is wrong with my body.

"No, you won't scream. You can't. I'm afraid you didn't take LSD, my little angel, but rather a compound a friend of mine, a genius chemist, created. You find yourself unable to move, yes? But your mind is wide awake and so is your nervous system." He laughs, a nasty, crackly sound. "No don't bother trying to nod, I think you'd find that rather impossible at the moment."

MOVE! Though I order my body nothing happens. I try to lift my arm, to move my fingers… nothing. But my eyes, those I can move. Why? I try to open my mouth, but it's frozen as well.

"We'll start with a finger."

I try to shake my head, to roll to my side and crawl away. Nothing. I can't even whimper. A tear falls from my eye followed by more until my vision is blurred. He lifts my hand so that it's in my line of sight. Before I realize his intentions, he slices through my index finger and middle finger with the knife. One swift motion. No pain. But only for a moment. Searing pain explodes from my hand, but I can't react or scream. He stares into my eyes as though studying my reaction. Blood spurts from the stumps, coating my hand and arm.

"Hmm, can't have you bleeding to death."

He grabs a strip from the shredded pillowcase and wraps it around my upper arm. With a pencil, he creates a crude tourniquet to control the bleeding. The pressure builds on my arm with each twist of the pencil until it snaps. Relief floods through me as the awful pressure is released. Short lived. When he turns his back to rifle through the closet, I urge my deadened body to move. Nothing, not even a twitch. My heart rate slows as the drug takes deeper hold on my body. Maybe I'll die, stop breathing. But no. My lungs continue to take in shallow breaths of air. The monster returns with a piece of wooden hanger and twists the tourniquet back in place.

"Now I'd like to know if the next fingers hurt the same, more, or less with the tourniquet in place," he says as he raises my hand up again. "Perhaps you can answer my questions with your eyes. We have lots of fingers and toes to work with before moving on. So plenty time to practice our communication."

I feel the knife cut through my ring and little fingers, but my eyes are too full of tears to see. I want to cry, to beg, but I'm frozen, unable to move or speak. Please let me pass out before he continues...

He wipes the tears from my eyes with a cloth. "Now, did that hurt more or less?" His brown eyes meet mine, and I try to look away but can't. "Oh well, let's try again."

His wickedly sharp knife slices through my thumb, and he holds my hand in front of my face so I can see the bloody stump. More tears fill my eyes and fall down my cheeks. Please stop, oh please, God, help me! Please... please... please...

"Does it hurt more or less when you see the damage?"

I try to close my eyes, but even that small comfort is denied me as my eyelids refuse to obey. He moves on to my left hand, and I try to float away, to go somewhere else, but every slice of the knife brings me back...

~

LOGAN

I'm just about finished sifting through the rubble in the family room when Mr. Kincaid returns from outside. Violent crashes shake the ceiling. It sounds like something is slamming large furniture into the floor over and over. For a moment I'm torn. My gaze flicks between Mr. Kincaid and the hall leading toward the stairs. Mom appears beside Mr. Kincaid, shaking her head, having sensed my inner turmoil. Once again, I give in to duty though my heart screams to ignore my head and go after Kacie.

"There are four more kids in here somewhere," Mr. Kincaid says as we enter the family room. "Blake found three upstairs. Those three and the two we just found are outside. They started as a group of nine." Nine... just like the tarot card.

"Maybe they fled?" Mom suggests as she fusses over me, looking for new injuries.

"I'm fine," I mutter.

"We'll need to do a complete sweep, down here first, then upstairs." Mr. Kincaid doesn't wait for a reply and heads toward the kitchen.

"Wait!" My tone comes out harsher than I intended, but I really hate being left in the dark. "Why can't Blake and Kacie sweep upstairs? Is she okay? What the hell's going on?" My voice rises with each question. "I'll kill Blake!"

"Stand down!" Mr. Kincaid yells. Though he tries to hide it, to remain professional, I can see the fear reflected in his eyes.

"Kacie..." I limp over the debris, making my way to the stairs as quickly as my lame knee will allow.

"Logan, you can't help," Mom says, grabbing my arm.

I wrench away. "Like hell I can't."

"Baby, you can barely climb the stairs." Mom tries her soothing tone on me, but it's a wasted effort. "Blake will keep her safe."

"Where have I heard that before, Mother?" I regret the words the moment they leave my traitorous mouth. But the damage is done. Tears fill Mom's eyes. "I-I'm sorry..."

"No, not now," she says before covering her mouth with her hand. Her slight frame shakes as she fights back the sobs I know threaten to consume her.

"Mom, I—"

She stares at the floor and takes a shaky breath. "I know it's been hard. Working with Blake, it bringing up memories. But you have to let it go. Neither of you were at fault. And now is certainly not the time to dig up the past."

"We need you down here, Logan," Mr. Kincaid says, laying a hand on my shoulder. "Let's finish our search and find those kids."

I nod. *Keep her safe, Blake.*

23
Building Tensions
~

KACIE

I wrench myself from the vision, unable to stomach seeing any more. Coughs rock my body, and I curl up in a ball trying to fight the overwhelming nausea. As my mind clears a bit, I realize that I'm lying on the floor with Blake's warm body wrapped behind me. I settle back into his warm embrace, biting my lip to stop my whimpers. The coughing subsides to be replaced by shivers. Blake sits up, pulling me with him so I'm cradled across his lap.

"Aww, the party was just getting started and you bailed," Tracy's spirit whispers in my ear.

I'm too spent to react. Good.

"Couldn't stomach it, huh?" Her voice shifts to my other ear, and this time I can't control the tremors betraying my fear.

"I…" My voice catches in my throat, so I just nod.

"What happened?" Blake asks, and I don't know if he's asking me, Tracy, or Chief Ken. "I thought it was just a vision."

Ken answers. "Powerful physical mediums like Kacie can have very real visions. I'm guessing she saw at least part of Tracy's murder. Probably felt it too."

"But it was so much more than a murder, wasn't it?" She directs the question at me, and all I can do is give a weak nod of my head. "Come, now, speak up." Her fake, cheery tone is so at odds with what I just saw. My stomach roils again. No wonder the ghost is insane.

"Torture," I murmur, burying my face against Blake's shoulder as though that might erase the images I saw, what I felt. "Tracy received the professor's full attention."

"While sweet, innocent Angela watched… and did *nothing*." Well I think that's a bit of an overstatement considering the fact that Angela was bound and gagged.

A few deep breaths later and a bit of my composure returns. "I'm sorry. I know that's inadequate considering the hell you experienced—"

She laughs, yet there is no humor at all. "Hell… yes. Did you know I relive the event constantly? I even have flashes of pain…"

"You need to know that Angela has suffered terribly as well."

"Has she now."

I realize my mistake when Tracy's spirit darkens, turning into a wispy black fog. I should've focused on her longer, on her suffering. Angry energy crackles, raising the hair on my arms. What she experienced, just the brief glimpse into it that I had was overwhelming. Now she thinks I'm understating her ordeal.

"Please, Tracy, I'm not trying to—"

"I think you've said enough for now."

A blast of frigid air rams into me. A tornado of swirling energy fills the room, picking up anything that isn't heavy enough to withstand the wind. Blake's arms tighten around me to the point of pain. I wrap my arms around his neck, hanging on with everything I have when that energy zeroes in on me. My hair whips around hiding my view of the furious ghost. The energy tugs at my body, trying to wrench me from Blake's arms. But Tracy doesn't know he isn't an ordinary human. His arms remain steel bands holding me against his chest. The wind picks his body up a few inches and slams it back down, jarring every bone in my body.

"Blake, let me go before she hurts you."

"Never." We bounce a few more times then fly across the room, ramming into the wall. Blake takes the impact full on his back.

"Tracy, please, let's talk. Tell me everything." I glance around but can't find Chief Ken. Where is he? Is he okay?

"Talk is so boring… this…" Her dark form looms inches from my face. I try not to react but I startle a bit anyway. She laughs, having received the reaction she obviously wanted. "This is so much more fun."

~

LOGAN

A scream pierces through the house as I'm poking through a coat closet. Kacie? I brace myself against the doorframe, my fingers digging into the wood. Blake will keep her safe becomes a repeated mantra in my head. I have a job to do. Besides, I know Kacie can take care of herself...

"Are you all right, honey?" Mom asks. "That wasn't Kacie's scream."

I nod without turning to look at her. "I know. The kids aren't hiding in here. Where to next?"

"There's no basement." It's Mr. Kincaid. His heels click on the wood floor as he paces. "We checked every closet, cabinet, and the garage. Nothing."

"Upstairs?" I ask as I force myself to unclench my jaw.

"Upstairs," Mr. Kincaid agrees.

Finally. I head to the staircase leading up into more darkness. My light sweeps the stairs revealing nothing but the blood-red stains left by our pranksters. The light doesn't reach the balcony which is cloaked in shadow. When I'm halfway up the stairs, a figure appears on the landing making my stomach drop to the floor. I shine the light on the figure, tensing when I see Chief Diving Eagle.

"Shouldn't you be with Kacie?" I ask unable to control the accusatory tone.

"She is with Blake." He levels a hard gaze at me. "She does battle with the spirit. Occupying her so we can search for the missing kids."

"She needs my help," I say when I reach the second story. I head down the hall toward her bright aura.

The chief's hand on my arm stops me. "We need your help. Kacie and Blake are fine together. You must trust them to handle the situation."

"Why do you need me? It's just a search and rescue."

"I feel there is more to it than that." The chief's gaze travels across the ceiling as though he's trying to see through the drywall and plaster. "I have a bad feeling. The kids are somewhere on the third floor. I don't think the angry spirit wishes for us to find them."

A loud *thud* echoes down the hallway from a room near the end. Silence follows. I resist the urge to head down the hall to make sure that Kacie's okay. Moans fill the air around us along with the sound of rattling chains.

"For the love of…" I trail off, looking for a sign of Tracy. Why is she resorting to cliché ghostly noises? Nobody could possibly be scared by—

"Help!"

"*Arrggh!*"

Human screams tear through the moaning and clinking chain sounds. I guess our intruders are afraid of old school ghost crap. It doesn't make much sense. As I follow the others up the second staircase, I can't help but wonder if the drama is a way to separate Kacie and me.

~

KACIE

The fierce wind dies down abruptly, and I brush the hair from my face. I see my reflection in the mirrored closet door. Dear God, I look like I was caught in a tornado with my hair sticking up all over the place. My skin is ashen, my eyes wide. I glance at Blake's reflection. He doesn't look much better. I've never seen his skin so pale. His arms are still wrapped around me to the point of pain. I'm going to have some lovely bruises tomorrow.

"She gone?" Blake asks in a whisper.

"For now." I send my aura out a bit, searching for anything unusual. "I don't feel anything."

"I guess we bored her." Blake pushes me to my feet. "There are still four kids in this house somewhere. We have five more rooms to search."

"I have a strange feeling… like we're missing something very important."

"Any idea what?"

"Where did the crime happen?" I pull out my phone and dial Rebecca, asking her the same question when she answers.

"Give me a minute…" Computer keys click in the background as Rebecca searches for the answer. "Um, we know it was upstairs because Amy fell down the stairs."

"Which floor? The house is three stories."

"Not in this picture it isn't," Rebecca says. "I'm looking at a two-story house here. The third story was added sometime after the crime."

"Thanks."

"I won't keep you," Rebecca says, her voice full of concern. "But you don't sound well. Let me know if you need anything."

I disconnect the call and shove the phone back into my pocket. Footsteps bang on the floor above us—the others looking for the stupid kids. But the real action won't take place there. I have a feeling that Tracy will want to confront me in the room where it all happened thirty years ago. Blake nods when I share my revelation.

"Do you know which room?" he asks as we head down the dark hall.

"No clue. I figured she'd help us find it."

More footsteps pound from above—several pairs of feet running, followed by a *thud*. Then silence. I push the next door open, shining my flashlight around, unsure what I'm looking for. It's just another normal room: beds, posters, dressers, books... nothing unusual.

"What did I expect to find? Blood stains on the wall?" Though I whispered it under my breath, Blake still heard me.

"Yeah, I doubt anyone would voluntarily live in a room covered in blood stains." He continues down the hall, then stops and backs up. Is he counting his paces? "Something's off here."

"What?" I look around the hall, unable to find anything odd.

"There's extra space here... like something was closed off."

I shine my light over the wall. It looks normal. A rectangular table sits in front of it, and several framed sorority photos hang on the light blue wall. I run my fingers over the paint. It isn't until I step back that I realize how long the table is—at least five or six feet long. Blake is right, it is odd, and yet...

"It's not wallpaper. Did you think we'd peel it back and find a door?" I laugh, but it comes out sounding more frightened than amused. "This isn't an Edgar Allan Poe story." As though on cue, Poe lands on the table, poking at his wing feathers with his beak. "And you're a crow not a raven," I tell the bird as he turns his red eyes on me.

"It wouldn't be that hard to drywall over a door."

"Well it's not like we can get sledgehammers and break through the wall to check."

Intense shivers rack my body. Oh, this isn't good at all. All of my instincts scream that there's something bad behind the wall. Just as I'm about to back away, a ghostly face emerges from the wall. Large and distorted, it warps and stretches like something out of a nightmare. I bite back a scream as the face morphs into a girl—Tracy.

"I see you found the party," she says. Her hysterical laughter sends more tremors through my body. "Don't leave yet. The fun hasn't even started."

She disappears, then pops back, enveloping me within her ethereal form. Iciness surrounds me seeping through my skin.

~

LOGAN

A scream cuts through the house, sending chills through me and raising the hair on my arms. Kacie—I'd recognize her voice anywhere. Why the hell isn't Blake doing a better job protecting her? I watch Mr. Kincaid usher two frightened middle-school boys toward the staircase, clenching my jaw to keep from yelling at them to move faster. They're frightened, I get it. But can't they move? You'd think they'd want out of this hell house, but the way those two drag their feet...

When I hear Blake shout something incomprehensible, I push past everyone, taking the stairs as fast as I can. The adults can find the remaining two kids. Pain lances through my leg, radiating from my swollen knee.

I grip the railing to keep from falling the last few steps. As I limp down the dark hallway, my eyes scan for any trace of my friends. There! Surrounded in dark gray mist. Blake holds Kacie against him, his arms straining as though playing tug-of-war. If that werewolf is straining, the force must be immense. Kacie thrashes around, her hair flying everywhere.

I freeze, unsure what to do. Rushing in full throttle could cause more harm than good. After watching the scene for a few more seconds, I shout, "Tracy!"

Blake flies backward and impacts the wall, Kacie still wrapped in his arms. The mist encircles me, the icy cold cutting through to my bones. I brace myself, waiting to be cast to the ceiling or thrown across the hall. Nothing. Tracy's spirit evaporates, leaving behind nothing but a chill lingering in the air.

"I've never been the object of tug-of-war before," Kacie murmurs, rubbing the back of her head. It must have banged against Blake's shoulder when he hit the wall.

"At least you weren't embedded in a wall," Blake says, eyeing the hole in the wall left by his body.

"I think I broke my head on your shoulder."

I pull Kacie to her feet, enfolding her in my arms. "Are you okay?"

"Thanks to Blake." She shivers in my embrace, wrapping her arms around me and clutching my back. "She keeps trying to possess me. Doesn't realize I've dealt with so much worse than her." She leans in close, her words barely a whisper. "She's really strong. I'm scared."

"Your skin is like ice." I place both palms on her pink cheeks, trying to warm her up.

"Yeah, I'm fine over here," Blake says as he pushes to his feet. "Don't mind the werewolf-sized hole in the wall."

Ignoring him, I lean down and kiss her cold nose as she continues to tremble in my arms. He stalks over to the other wall, shoving a long table out of the way. It flies down the hall, landing on its side. Looks like Tracy managed to piss off Blake—not like it's that hard or anything.

"She got all pissy when I said I'd break down this wall," he says, knocking on the wood. "I think that's just what I'll do."

"I thought she wanted to lead us to the place she died," Kacie says, stepping away. My arms fall to my sides as she moves to the wall, running her fingers along the paint. "But I think she was protecting it, keeping us away for some reason."

Loud crashes bang from downstairs one after the other. When we don't move or react, more banging, crashing, and thudding follows.

"See, she's trying to distract us." Kacie knocks on the wall. "It's like she's throwing a tantrum… What could be behind here that she wants to protect so badly?"

Kacie's phone rings.

"You're on speaker, Rebecca. What did you find out?"

"Tracy was cremated. Her remains are in a mausoleum at Haven Head Cemetery. I mean it's not like we'd go dig up a grave anyway, but that's definitely not an option here."

"You don't actually dig up graves do you?" Blake asks with wide eyes.

"No, of course not." I snap at him. "This isn't a TV show. Can you imagine us in a graveyard in the middle of the night with shovels? Please... besides, modern caskets are sealed and you need equipment to get them out. We'd need a court order."

"Sorry," Blake says, his voice dripping sarcasm. "I'm not our resident ghost expert."

"It's okay, Blake. It sounds like Logan's overdue for his pain meds," Rebecca says. I bite my tongue to keep the nasty retort at bay. Hell, she's right... I am overdue for some pain relief.

"If she was cremated, then anything could be tying her spirit here," Kacie says still eyeing the wall as though it contains lost secrets.

"It doesn't really matter, though," Rebecca says. "I think banishment through burning is the same as an exorcism. And I hate to think where she might end up if she's exorcised."

Blake shakes his head. "Wait, cremation *is* burning."

"Thanks, Rebecca," Kacie says before disconnecting the call. "Cremation sets the spirit free. If a spirit is tied to our plane and we force it to leave through burning, then it's a bit different."

"How so?"

"We perform a brief exorcism rite before burning an object we think ties a spirit here."

"I don't understand—"

I cut off the conversation. "We don't have time for this bullshit."

"He needs to understand," Kacie says, laying her hand on my arm. "Whether a spirit realizes it or not, they are using dark magic or forces to tie their consciousness here. When we burn the thing tying them, it severs that magic. Rebecca's doing some fascinating research on this. I'm sure she'd be thrilled to share."

"Good enough." Blake grins. "Now, can I smash through this wall?"

"One minute." I pull out my phone to call Mr. Kincaid. When he answers, I don't waste time. "We think there's a hidden room. Can Blake tear down the wall?"

"Well? Can I?"

"You're entirely too excited about this. Mr. Kincaid's on his way up."

As we're waiting for approval, Blake sizes up the wall, making a big show of it... probably to annoy me. Damn but it works. I need to do a better job controlling my emotions around him. The last thing I want is for him to have any insight into my feelings. It's hard to believe we were best friends five years ago. The memory brings images I'd prefer remain buried, and I clamp it down deep within me. I refuse to allow Tracy to use these memories against me...

Blake looks at me with inscrutable eyes. He knows what I'm thinking. His throat convulses as he swallows hard. I shake my head, and he goes back to his exploration of the wall. I feel a light tap on my arm. Glancing at Kacie, I try to ignore the question in her eyes. She saw the exchange, but I'm not ready to share—not yet, and certainly not here.

24

Tear Down that Wall

~

KACIE

Such an odd exchange between Logan and Blake. Something big happened between them. But I can't ask with a memory-stealing, emotion-abusing ghost lurking nearby. With the two of them working together so often now, it will come out—probably sooner rather than later.

Footsteps pound on the stairs making me tense for a moment. Our resident spirit has been quiet for a few minutes. Regrouping? Waiting? I release my aura, searching for anything unusual. Nothing. No cold spots or lurking shadows. My pulse races along with my vibrating bracelet. The only reminder that darkness lurks nearby. A breeze wafts down the hall, and I whip my head around looking for the source. Dark shadows dance on the ceiling for a second or two before disappearing. Were they even there? She has me jumping at shadows and wind.

Maybe Blake and Logan have the right idea. I've never seen anyone find a wall so interesting.

"What's this about breaking down walls?" Mr. Kincaid asks as he rushes up, swinging a bright camping lantern. The light bobs with his steps, creating more eerie shadows on the walls and ceiling.

"The dimensions are off." Blake makes a sweeping gesture at the wall. "I think there's a room behind here."

Now I watch three guys knock on the wall and scrutinize it likes it's the most fascinating thing on the planet.

"You sure?" Mr. Kincaid asks.

"Only one way to find out," I say, pushing Logan and Blake aside. "Hey, Tracy, I'm busting through this wall. How does that make you feel?" Before I can take a breath to taunt her again, something plows into me, sending me flying down the hall.

"Crap! Are you okay?" Logan asks when he reaches my side.

"Yeah. Rug burn doesn't hurt nearly as much as road rash."

Blake pulls me to my feet. "There must be easier ways... or do you just like getting tossed around, princess?"

"Why do you keep calling me princess?"

He bites his lip and gazes at me with a rather guilty expression. "Sorry… it's just… that play you were in back in sixth grade…"

"I don't remember you in sixth grade."

"I didn't go to your school, but I went to the play with Logan's family to see Daniel." He shrugs, looking rather sheepish. "You made quite an impression on twelve-year-old me as the fairy princess. Even now when I look at you, I see her."

His frank admission leaves me speechless. I'm saved from commenting when the pictures Blake had removed from the wall rise from the floor and hover for a moment before flying at us. I duck waiting for impact. A loud crash of breaking glass and wood explodes around me, but nothing hits me. When I straighten up, Blake is shaking glass from his hair. He shielded me from the flying debris.

"Thanks." I pick several long, wood slivers from the back of his flannel shirt.

"You okay?" Logan asks.

Blake chuckles. "It'll take more than a few small pictures to hurt me."

"Um, those weren't exactly what I'd call small." I kick at a thick piece of wood that landed next to my foot. "I think I'd be in the hospital."

"You do wind up there a lot," Logan says with a nervous laugh.

I glare at him. "You're one to talk."

"Let's tear this wall down, shall we," Mr. Kincaid says with a hint of glee in his voice.

Ugh. What is it with guys and destruction?

As they huddle together to discuss the most expedient way to break through, I wander the hallway, watching shadows gather and disperse in the lantern light. There's a steady pattern to the ebb and flow, like a heartbeat or breathing. My footsteps crunch as I walk through the shattered photos, quietly watching for Tracy's reaction to the impending destruction of the wall. Energy crackles in the air, making the tiny hairs on my arm stand on end. Adrenaline shoots through me. She's about to manifest.

"Duck!" I shout.

Though I have no clue where the attack will come from, I do know it's coming. They act immediately on my words and crouch down just in time. A door torn from its hinges flies over them, smashing into the wall just inches from their heads. Plaster and drywall dust fill the air, making it hard to breathe. I cover my nose with my hand, trying not to choke on the grit.

"What the effing hell!" Blake shouts as he picks up the remains of the large wood door and tosses it further down the hall.

"Language!" Mr. Kincaid snaps through coughs.

"I said effing not—"

"Stop." Mr. Kincaid removes his glasses and cleans them on his shirt. "We need to focus, regroup."

"There's no time," I cry, feeling the energy spiking again. "We go in now or get out of here. She's coming back for more."

Mr. Kincaid whips his phone out. "Marianne, I need you and the others to start with plan B. It should get the spirit riled up enough to leave us alone... or at least spread out her energy." Silence fills the hall as he listens to her response. "No I haven't seen anything, but she's throwing stuff around here like a child having a tantrum. I think we found something and we need a distraction."

~

LOGAN

I want to grab the phone from Mr. Kincaid, to make sure Mom is okay. She's so open and empathic, I can't help but worry a nasty ghost like Tracy might try to hurt her. But I retain my professionalism... somehow. Plan B involves the start of an exorcism ritual—sealing a bag of spirit-repelling herbs in the walls at the four cardinal points: north, south, east, and west. That will piss off Tracy, and hopefully keep her off our backs while we break down the wall. It isn't safe for Mom though.

My fingers brush the phone in my pocket. I know I shouldn't distract her, but I want to warn her. I don't think she's ever encountered a spirit as vicious as this one. *She knows.* Like a premonition or a vision, I feel the truth. By calling her I'd draw Tracy's attention right to her. Unwise. I can tell the moment they start. The hallway warms up at least ten degrees, signaling Tracy's exit.

"I need this," I murmur to Kacie as I slip my leather jacket from her shoulders.

I hand the jacket to Blake. He shrugs it on without comment.

"Be careful," Kacie calls out to Blake who turns and grins at her.

"The wall is no match for me, princess."

He smashes his elbow into the drywall several times. Once there are some new holes, he grabs pieces in his hands and wrenches them from the wall. Piece by piece a small mound forms at his feet.

"I need a hammer or a crowbar," he mutters, looking over his shoulder.

"How about we not introduce a deadly weapon with a sadistic ghost hanging around?" My words come out sharper than I intended.

"Logan?"

I glance over my shoulder at Kacie. Her face is scrunched into that adorable pout she gets when she's confused about something. My shoulders slump and I hold my arms out to her. She buries her face in my neck as she cuddles in my embrace. I draw from her quiet strength while breathing in the light scent of vanilla in her hair. A few deep breaths later and I'm much calmer.

"Sorry." I release Kacie and step forward to help Blake. "You think we can pull these boards off, the two of us?"

He nods. "We may end up with splinters, but I suppose that's better than a flying crowbar to the head."

Kacie grabs my arm. "Wait, you're injured… or have you already forgotten?" Her voice is teasing but her eyes serious.

"I'll do it," Mr. Kincaid says as he rolls up one sleeve then the other. "I'm not much use for anything else."

Loud *thumps* explode from the stairs leading down to the main floor. Chunks of the wooden railing scatter across the landing. Crap. We need to finish this and fast before Tracy tears the house down.

"Hold that end while I pull this one," Blake says, grabbing onto a board blocking the hidden door.

Mr. Kincaid pushes on the board while Blake yanks on the other end. The wood splinters and cracks as the nails are pulled from the doorjamb. Once the board is off, Mr. Kincaid steps back, running a hand over his forehead.

"Maybe you were right," Mr. Kincaid says in a strained voice. "Perhaps a crowbar—"

"Nah, I got it now." Blake yanks two more boards free. "Now that they aren't blocked it's much easier."

Pieces of wood fly as Blake continues pulling planks away from the door. He grunts and strains but the boards are no match for the brute strength of a werewolf. The last board is freed and he staggers back, falling on his ass. He blows the hair out of his eyes before tossing the last piece aside. Laughing, he leans back on his elbows.

"That was more of a workout than I expected," he says, huffing a bit. "Someone really didn't want us getting into that room."

Kacie stares at him with wide eyes. "I had no idea just how strong you are." She tips her head, studying him with an odd expression. "It's… disconcerting."

"I'd never hurt you, princess." He rises from the floor in a fluid motion, more like flowing water than human. "A werewolf is good to have around," he adds, handing my jacket back to her.

"I'm beginning to see that," she murmurs, her eyebrows raised like she hasn't decided yet. She takes the jacket and busies herself by sweeping off the plaster dust with her fingers. After she slips it on, she meets my gaze, unsure and nervous.

"We're stalling," I say, holding my hand out to her. "Ready?"

She nods, placing her chilled hand in mine. I push her behind me and lead the way through the mysterious doorway.

～

KACIE

I don't know what I expected… but this isn't it. The room is musty, tickling my nose with the stale copper aroma of blood. I sneeze several times and rub my nose with my hand. The flashlight beam bounces around the small room revealing two twin beds, a dresser, two nightstands, a bookcase—standard college room fare. A torn Rolling Stones poster droops from one wall. The carpet is shag, either cream or white, hard to tell in this light. What isn't hard to see? A massive dark stain on the carpet in the middle of the room. Based on the smell, it must be blood. Tracy's.

"My God," Blake says in an odd nasal voice. When I glance back at him, he has his nose pinched shut. Werewolf senses. Almost forgot. It must smell awful to him. "Didn't they even bother cleaning?"

Mr. Kincaid steps through the doorway and does a quick scan of the room. "It looks like they just boarded it up rather than trying to clean."

"Eww." My stomach roils with my words. It's just sick on so many levels. "Why?"

"Better question," Logan says, skirting around the dark stain on the floor. "Why is this room the only one in the house not wrecked?"

"You're right." I follow him to the dresser and sift through the papers on top. Nothing but concert posters and ticket stubs. These girls liked music. "You'd think Tracy's anger would be focused on this room, yet she hasn't touched it… why?"

"She can't come in here," Logan says his eyes darting around the room.

"Again, why?"

Logan shakes his head. "She's the only one who can answer that."

"Uh, I think..." Blake trails off, motioning his head toward the open doorway. "Here's your chance."

Her energy is cleaner, less murky—due to the start of the exorcism or our discovery of the room, I don't know. She floats, a gray misty shape, watching, waiting. Our gazes lock as her form slowly bobs up and down in time with my breathing. Whatever I say or do next is critical. She's on the cusp, hovering between good and evil. Confusion is apparent in her fathomless eyes.

"Come, in, Tracy," I say, beckoning her forward with a wave of my hand. "Please, let's talk."

She shies away, and I pull back, lowering my hand to my side. *Is this the same girl who pinned Raven to the ceiling and broke my boyfriend?* Her energy wavers, beginning to fade.

"Wait!" Logan says, taking a step toward her.

I grab his arm, holding him beside me. "Please, wait."

"They're exorcising me," Tracy says in a small, plaintive tone so unlike her prior attitude.

"What did you expect?" I ask, shrugging. "We warned you, begged you to cross over, to move on."

"But... but..."

Blake leans forward, his words a whisper. "It's a trick."

He reveals the truth my mind wanted to hide. Like the words held magic, now I can see the sneer on her face, the plotting behind her eyes. I wanted to help her so badly that it blinded me. Maybe it was the vision, my desire for her to finally be at peace.

"Come join us," Logan says in a pleasant, even tone. Points for him, I want to scream at her.

Blake chuckles, yet there's no humor in the dry laugh. "Can't, can you. Barred from your death site?"

"You know nothing!" Tracy spits out the words as her form solidifies. One moment she's an ethereal gray mist, and the next she looks alive. "You aren't even human."

Blake blinks several times. "Was that supposed to be an insult?" He stares at her for several seconds. "You got a little..." He points at the bloody stains covering her clothes.

"Animal!" Tracy screams, her hair flying around her.

"You have no idea," Blake says with a cruel smile.

She shrieks and flies toward him but is stopped by an invisible barrier. Her body bounces backward as energy crackles around us. The barrier seems to drain her energy, leaving her more subdued. Rising to her feet, she glares at us, still in her death clothes but not quite her death state.

"Want to see it?" she asks, staring at me, reading my mind.

"No." I swallow around a hard lump forming in my throat. "I saw enough in my vision. I know you suffered terribly, and I am so sorry."

"You. Can't. Even. Begin. To understand. My pain." She emphasizes every syllable, her bloodshot eyes never leaving mine.

~

LOGAN

I sense movement, and in the next moment Tracy throws herself at the barrier, a screaming, howling banshee. She fights against the magic barring her. Static electricity sparks through the room, zooming around, visible in the darkness. I push Kacie behind me as the manic ghost continues her relentless assault on the barrier. A deafening *boom* reverberates through the room, followed by a wave of energy. I push Kacie down, falling on top of her to shield her from the ghost's wrath. Pain lances up my back like thousands of cat claws, making me cry out both in shock and pain. I glance back—Samson and Delilah hiss their displeasure at Tracy, their claws digging into my back.

The claws retract when I yell at them, and all the other pain surfaces. Ignoring the throbbing in my ribs, I roll to my side to free Kacie, sending the cats leaping away. Tracy lets out one last anguished wail before slumping and falling to the floor. My familiars circle her prone body, mouths open, scenting the air. The heaviness in the air lessens, but I continue to take in shallow breaths to keep from aggravating the pain. I watch Tracy, searching for… well not signs of life, but existence? Her form flickers like an old movie, and I wonder if she'll just wink out of existence.

"Is she…" Blake trails off, pushing himself up on his elbows. "That was quite a blast. You both okay?"

"Yeah," Kacie says, rubbing her head. "Where's Mr. Kincaid?"

"Out here," Mr. Kincaid says from the hall. "I got out just before the explosion."

"Logan…" Kacie pulls on my arm while pointing at Tracy's prone form. "I've never seen, I mean, she can't…"

"Her spirit would've disappeared if she was destroyed." I try to struggle to my feet but give up, sagging back down. Kacie leans against me, and I wrap my arms around her.

Blake eyes us. "You two are not okay."

"When Tracy forced the barrier, she released a lot of psychic energy," I say, resting my cheek on Kacie's head.

"It drained all of us, not just her," Kacie adds.

"I feel fine," Blake says stretching his arms over his head.

"Yeah, why is that?" I ask, unable to hide the genuine surprise from my voice.

"Rebecca will be thrilled," Kacie says.

Blake raises his brows. "Why, she like stamina?"

Kacie giggles. "Get your mind out of the gutter, Blake. She likes researching puzzles."

"Oh, no. I ain't no one's guinea pig."

Tracy's spirit releases a soft sigh, like a light exhale of breath... if ghosts could breathe. She floats to her feet as though controlled by invisible strings. Still solid, her dark eyes scan the room. A smile crosses her face when she realizes that she made it through the psychic barrier. All I can do is stare at the ghost and wonder what that mysterious smile means. Maybe she's as drained as we are. Kacie squeezes my hand, her aura flickering from exhaustion. I meet her gaze. Evade and stall for time to recover—I try to send the message to her in my expression.

"Now that you're in here, love," Blake says, gesturing at the room. "Care to share why you wanted in so bad?"

Tracy blushes at Blake's obvious flirting. I had no idea a spirit could blush, even one who appears as human as she does. I mean, it takes blood to blush, right. More manipulation? She glides to one of the beds and reaches out to it. Her hand goes straight through. When she tries again, she lets out a frustrated growl as her hand once again passes through the mattress.

"I can't touch anything?" she says, her words sounding more like a question than a statement.

One moment she's by the bed and the next she appears inches from Blake's face. He doesn't flinch, which I have to admit is rather impressive. I'm pretty sure even I'd have reacted to her sudden appearance.

"Are you really a werewolf?" she asks, leaning so close they'd touch were she human.

"Yep." Blake manages a blank face as the ghost circles him.

"Shift for me."

"It ain't a full moon, love," he says, shrugging his shoulders. I'm well aware that Blake can shift whenever he wants. He's a born alpha werewolf, not a bite victim. Blake's features take on a look of complete innocence. Damn but he can rival Kacie and Daniel in the acting department. "Why're you deflecting attention from that bed? What's under that mattress?"

"Nothing," she says, backing away, shaking her head furiously.

"Now we both know that ain't the truth." Blake saunters over to the bed and lifts the mattress.

"No!"

"Now what have we here?" Blake tosses a small book to me.

I open the book and flip through the pages. "It's a journal."

"It's mine!" Tracy howls, making a grab for the book. But her hand passes through. She may have enough power left to look almost human, but not enough to manipulate physical objects.

Kacie takes the book, hugging it to her chest. "This is very private, but it could also be what's keeping you from moving on."

Tracy's form flickers and sinks to the floor. She returns to an ethereal, misty spirit, and I can't help but notice how much lighter she is now than before. Swirling white and light gray misty energy compose her figure, a sure sign that she's close to acceptance of her fate.

"I'll talk, but just to you," she says, pointing at Kacie.

"No," I say, unwilling to leave Kacie alone with this dangerous adversary.

"Of course," Kacie says, directing a glare at me.

25

The Truth

~

KACIE

The boys follow Mr. Kincaid to the stairs but not without a lot of grumbling. Once they've disappeared from sight, I glance back at Tracy. She sighs, and her ghostly shoulders slump.

"That journal..." She trails off as tears fall from her eyes. She sniffs. "I-I... I reveal my relationship with Jeffrey in there."

"Jeffrey?"

"Associate Professor Jeffrey Rosenthal," she says, staring at the ground.

"The guy who ki—" I stop short before saying *killed you.*

"Yes. The man who murdered me."

I stare at her, in shock. "I don't know what to say."

I bite the inside of my cheek to keep from yelling or crying or... I don't know. What she said, I just don't know how to process it. I'm in way over my head here. And yet, I'm the only one who can help her. *What do I say?* I must wait too long to speak, or she can see the shock and aversion on my face.

"Aren't you going to say anything? Tell me how awful I am?"

"I don't know your story, and even if I did, it's not my place to judge." I lean against the bed, letting my head fall back against it. "One thing I do know. It seems that the professor may have had the psychic power of persuasion."

"What do you mean?" Her face fills with hope. It makes my stomach turn.

"I know someone who can manipulate her voice to convince people to do or think things." The image of Dr. Hayes fills my mind. Our resident Circle doctor not only has the power of persuasion, but she's dating my father... may become my mother soon. Her power scares me. Dad is oblivious, but she wants to tell him. What a can of worms to open...

"I didn't know that was possible," Tracy says, the hope fading from her eyes.

"You'll believe Blake's a werewolf, and I can obviously communicate with the dead, but someone who can persuade people is beyond belief?"

"Everyone can see me."

"You, sure. You're very powerful for a spirit. Most ghosts, not so much."

The conversation brings back memories best left buried—my mother and father fighting about my *delusions*, my mother running out because she couldn't deal with my emerging abilities, and worst of all, her admission that she too is psychic. I try to tamp them down, pretend it's all in the past. But it isn't. *Mother* wants to come visit, to reconnect after six years. I clench my jaw. Now isn't the time. Why do thoughts of her always crop up when I'm weakest?

"I'm sorry," Tracy says. Not sarcastic, not nasty, just a normal apology. "Your thoughts about your mother. You were projecting them rather loud. That's my talent, in life and death. I can read thoughts, um, the negative ones anyway. That's why I liked Jeffrey so much. His mind was closed to me for some reason. It was a relief to be around someone who wasn't broadcasting his thoughts all the time."

"That would suck." I let out a wry laugh. Of all powers, that's one I definitely wouldn't want. Mine isn't easy to deal with, seeing ghosts that others can't, but at least I can't hear everyone's thoughts. Hell, it's hard enough dealing with the nasty words thrown at me sometimes, I can't imagine hearing the negative thoughts too. At least it explains how she and her cronies knew our deep, dark secrets.

"Yeah, the one person whose thoughts I needed to read, I couldn't." She laughs but it turns into what sounds like a strangled sob. "I was so happy about it too." She pauses, staring up at the ceiling. "I loved him, you know."

"I'm sorry. I know what it's like to be betrayed by someone you love."

"I know. That's why I wanted to talk to you."

I watch her fidget, wringing her fingers together. "Tell me what happened, why you're so afraid."

"It was supposed to be Angela," she whispers, her eyes downcast.

I stare at her, trying to keep the shock from my face, from my thoughts. She knew, but so did Angela. Maybe I'm jumping to conclusions. Maybe Tracy didn't know exactly what the psycho professor had planned.

"Tell me," I say, my voice calm and even.

"Jeffrey was a master manipulator. I knew that... but I loved him anyway. Ours was a secret romance. He would've lost his job if anyone knew he was involved with a student."

"Did you know about him and Angela?"

She stares at the wall, probably sorting through memories, the kind best forgotten. I watch in silence as she glides back and forth across the room, inches above the floor. Her face morphs through several different expressions, none of them happy.

"I found o-out," she says, her voice cracking. "I blamed her, not him. Now looking back, I think he had lots of other girls, lots of stupid, naïve puppets."

"From what I read about him and what came out in the trial, that wouldn't surprise me."

"What happened in the trial?"

"Not until you tell me what happened that night."

A smirk spreads across her face. "Well, see, I'm rather impatient and tired of pretending."

"Pretending?"

She doesn't answer. One moment everything is calm and the next her spirit energy slams into me, knocking the air from my lungs. As I struggle to breathe, she worms her way into my body. Having a vision is one thing—our consciousness merges for a few minutes. But this... this is something entirely different. Damn her. She only pretended to be affected by the psychic drain caused by the barrier breaking. And stupid me... I fell for it.

"Get out," I hiss through my clenched teeth, unable to make a sound louder than a whisper.

Again no answer. Painful convulsions rack my body. I fall to my side, my fingers digging into the plush carpet. A strange sensation pours down my arms, like cold slime running through my veins. When I try to lift my arm it remains unmoving. Panic surges, my heart racing so loud my pulse roars in my ears. The icy, slimy sensation oozes throughout my body, down my legs and into my feet. My bracelet vibrates on my wrist, moving up and down, slamming against the bone in my wrist. I concentrate on the bracelet, hoping to draw strength from the antique silver. Though it never stops vibrating, it also doesn't stop the insidious ooze.

I won't let you! I scream in my head, unable to speak the words aloud.

You have no choice. The voice echoes in my mind. *Your body is mine now. Thanks.*

Frigid ooze spreads to my head, and I try to thrash around, to fight it, but my body refuses to move. I let out a muted sob when my body pushes up to kneel before the floor-length mirror. My hand picks up the flashlight, shining it at the mirror. I relive that moment in my vision when I… I mean Tracy… couldn't move due to the paralytic, trapped completely in my mind. But this isn't a medicine that will wear off. This is a complete possession. I can't. I won't allow this.

Get out! Get out! GET OUT! I visualize pushing the slimy ooze away. Picture it receding to disappear completely. Nothing. A malevolent cackle echoes in my head, bouncing around and rattling my teeth.

You can't stop me. You can't stop me. Over and over she sings the taunt. I stare into the mirror, trying to twitch a finger, my nose, my lips. Nothing. Complete darkness envelopes me as I'm pushed into a small corner of my mind, trapped within my own body. Though terror tries to seize what's left of me, I force myself to remain calm. I start counting backwards from one hundred, gathering my will and strength. From my dark corner, I watch Tracy test my body, flexing my arms and legs before twirling on my toes. She laughs and I wait in silence.

I keep counting, slowly pulling on her psychic energy which she seamlessly merged with my body—just a tiny bit at a time so she won't notice. Doubts plague my mind, what-ifs swirling around like vicious eels prowling in the dark waters. I tamp down my rabid fear and concentrate on the slow count backward. Eighty-two, eighty-one, eighty… When I reach "one" she *will* be evicted. I warned her. Bigger baddies have tried to possess me and failed…

~

LOGAN

It's so damn quiet up there. I pace the floor, not bothering to kick the shattered pieces of glass out of the way. The crunching of my footsteps is oddly soothing. Maybe I shouldn't have left her alone with Tracy. What if this is all some plan to get Kacie alone? I limp up a few stairs. Kacie appears at the top, a look of relief on her face.

"What happened? Everything okay? You okay?"

She laughs, bright and cheery. "So many questions." Giggles erupt as she bounds down the stairs, jumping into my arms. I catch her, barely keeping my footing.

"Crap." I cry out as my ribs scream in protest.

"What's the matter?" she asks, wrapping her arms around my neck.

"Injured. Remember?"

"Hmm, my poor, injured knight," she whispers against my lips, pulling me into a kiss.

The moment her lips meet mine, I know for sure. This isn't my Kacie. A war rages in my brain as I allow Tracy to kiss me. How did this happen? My stomach roils. Though it's Kacie's mouth on mine, the mere fact that it isn't really *her* makes me want to push her away, but I can't let on quite yet that I know. When she tries to deepen the kiss, I pull away, pretending to need a desperate breath while trying not to gag.

I stare into hazel eyes that I know so well, furious to see a light in them that isn't right. As she leans in for another kiss, I pull her into a hug. Blake moves in behind her, and I meet his disturbed gaze. He sniffs the air, his lips pulled back in a grimace. I nod my agreement.

"Kacie?" Blake says, tapping her back with his finger. He holds his arms open like he wants a hug. Tracy pulls away from me and throws herself into Blake's waiting arms.

She snuggles against him for a moment, but when she tries to pull away, he doesn't release her.

"Get out of me!" Kacie screams as she thrashes in Blake's iron grip. "Out. Out! OUT!"

A good sign. Kacie is fighting the possession. The adults all run into the room together, staring, mouths agape as Kacie struggles in Blake's arms.

"We need to perform an exorcism," Pastor Emilio says, clutching his Bible to his chest.

"No," Mom says, stepping between him and Kacie. "It's too dangerous. Kacie is strong. Let her fight." She turns to me. "How did this happen?"

I tell her about the psychic barrier, the booming wave of energy, and how our psychic powers were drained away.

"We thought Tracy was drained too, I mean, she acted like she was," I say, hanging my head. "She... Tracy looked so sad. We left them alone together when Tracy said she'd only talk to Kacie. I thought she was safe, and we were just around the corner on the stairs."

"It's my fault," Blake says in a strained voice as he wrestles with Kacie. "I wasn't as drained... I should've been—"

"Stop." Mom shakes her head. "It's no one's fault. We all take on risks with what we do."

"*Argh!*" Kacie screams. "Get out of my body!"

An explosion of psychic energy erupts from her, sending Blake flying backward still holding her in his arms. He slams against the wall and collapses to the floor. Kacie crumples against him, her eyes closed. Seconds tick by in silence as we wait to see what will happen. Blake sits up, cradling Kacie's limp body on his lap. Moaning, she rubs her forehead with her hand before trying to push away from Blake.

"Hold on, princess." Blake cups her cheek, turning her face so he can look in her eyes. "How are you feeling?"

"Fine. Let me go."

He grins. "How about a kiss first."

"In your dreams, wolf boy," Kacie says, mimicking Raven.

I fall to my knees beside her, ignoring the pain throbbing up my thigh. "You're back." She holds her arms out, and I pull her to me, cradling her face in my palms. "I was worried." Her lips meet mine, and I almost cry in relief. The kiss is sweet and tender, nothing like the aggressiveness of that harpy who possessed her.

"How did you know?" she asks, leaning her forehead against mine.

"Your eyes, your kiss. She just wasn't you." I kiss her cheek then her lips one last time. "It was awful seeing someone else looking out of your eyes."

"Glad you're back," Blake says, patting her shoulder. His lips curl into a smirk. "Just kidding about the kiss. I wouldn't poach your girl."

I laugh. "No, you were right. Great way to tell if Kacie was back in control."

"Enough fooling around," Pastor Emilio all but yells. "This isn't a playdate. We need to exorcise this ghost."

Mr. Kincaid clears his throat. "Pastor, would you mind checking on your assistant and the kids outside? We'll call you back if we need to start an exorcism."

"If you had listened to me to begin with, that evil being would be gone by now," the pastor says, his face turning dark red.

"Please, Emilio, let's head outside." Mr. Kincaid heads to the front door without looking back. Mom gives the pastor a little push on the back when he doesn't move. With a loud, obnoxious exhale, the pastor follows Mr. Kincaid out of the house.

"I think our dear pastor has become a bit overzealous," Mom says once he has left the room. "Now, Kacie, what do we need to do to move this poor girl on?"

"She's hiding and really weak now." Kacie's eyes dart around the room, searching. "I think she's ready to move on."

"Take the lead, dear," Mom says, motioning to Kacie.

I feel Kacie try to extend her aura, but she's too weakened by the psychic blast and the possession. She releases a loud breath and closes her eyes.

"I feel you nearby, Tracy," Kacie calls out. "When you possessed me it went both ways. I got all of your memories, your fear, and your guilt. I forgive you. For hurting Logan and Daniel, for what you did to me. I can't speak for your friends, but if they could forgive Angela, I think they'll forgive you too. You were young and in love—under the hypnotic spell of a very evil man. I felt the pull he had on you. It wasn't natural. He used you."

"I helped." Tracy's voice echoes around so it's impossible to pinpoint her position.

"You were coerced and used. You were a victim in so many ways..." Kacie trails off, her voice breaking a bit. She sniffs and her eyes fill with tears. "I was there, in your head, your memories. I felt the betrayal and the pain, but I also felt the love. It's time for you to move on. You've suffered enough. Forgive yourself. Go into the light."

Tracy gasps. "Oh, I see it. It's beautiful. Light green. Shouldn't it be white?"

"It's different for everyone," I say, taking a few steps forward. What I wouldn't give to see that light. "Move toward it."

"It's so warm. I hear water rushing. It smells clean and fresh." Her voice is filled with wonder, and my heart aches just a bit. Jealousy?

"Goodbye, Tracy," Kacie says, waving. "May you finally rest in peace."

"Thank you, all of you," Tracy says, her voice thick as though she's crying. "I don't deserve your kindness, and I don't think I deserve this beautiful light."

"If you didn't deserve it, it wouldn't be there," I call out, willing her to move on.

"Goodbye," she calls out.

Then she's gone. The heavy pressure in the house dissipates like it just exhaled. Kacie turns to me, silent tears trickling down her cheeks. I pull her into my arms, whispering soothing platitudes. There's nothing I can say to ease her pain right now, so I say a bit of everything. Possession is painful, and I'm sure Tracy's memories were much more traumatic than most.

She trembles in my arms, violent tremors. Though Poe lands on her shoulder cooing softly, she doesn't seem to notice the presence of her familiar. My cats wind around her ankles, mewing in unison. Even Blake steps forward and leans into her back, massaging her shoulders with rhythmic motions. We're a team; we'll help her through this.

26
Revelations

∽

KACIE

Though I managed to avoid a trip to the ER, Dr. Hayes still prescribed bed rest for two days. No ifs, ands, or buts. That means Dad and Gavin hovering by my bedside for a full forty-eight hours. At least we learned something important from this whole fiasco. Extreme psychic drain causes dehydration, so I have to suffer an IV drip as well. Dad was distraught because I got hurt in the line of duty again, and he carted the TV from my room—like I let the ghost attack me on purpose and need to be punished or something. No satellite, no Netflix, no Playstation, only time to sit and relive Tracy's memories over and over again.

Since Dad's blaming Logan and Blake for my condition, they've been temporarily banned until he settles down. No amount of pleading or whining will change anything so I revolt with the silent treatment. Night-time is the worst. Whenever I close my eyes, I see what happened to the girls like a horror movie in my mind. The nightmares once I'm asleep are even worse.

"No!" I awaken to my own fevered shout, thrashing around beneath my covers. Cool fingers brush the hair from my forehead. I gasp in a breath ready to fight.

"Shh," Logan whispers, brushing a kiss on my cheek. "It's okay, I'm here now."

I throw my arms around his neck and nuzzle against his shoulder. My breathing slows as he holds me in a tight embrace, driving away the shadows lurking in my mind. He buries his hand in my hair, massaging my head and the nape of my neck. The rest of the panic subsides, and I sag into his body, relief flooding me. After a few more minutes, he unwinds my arms from his neck and checks the IV stuck in my left hand. Lucky for me, I didn't pull it out. Dim light shines from the open bathroom door, enough that I can make out his features and the concern etched all over his face. Our eyes meet. I reach up, running a light caress across his cheek, and his deep frown lines disappear.

"How'd you get in here?" I thought Dad and Gavin had this place on lockdown.

"Your brother was worried," Logan says as he eases me back down on the bed. "He said you're having nightmares. You woke up screaming five times last night. I'm going to hold you tonight while you sleep. Keep the nightmares at bay."

"Thank you."

Tears fill my eyes, and I swallow hard. I won't allow them to fall. Not again. I roll over onto my side, and Logan curls up behind me, pulling me back against his chest. Closing my eyes, I fall asleep listening to his steady, rhythmic breathing.

～

"Morning, princess," Blake says, waking me from a sound sleep.

I roll over looking for Logan, but he's gone. Rubbing my eyes, I gape at Blake wondering not only how he got in my room but why he's here. Bright sunlight floods the room as he opens the curtains on both windows. Stretching my arms over my head, I yawn while testing the sore spots all over my body. Not too bad. I still have bruises from a few collisions with a wall or two, but the pain is a manageable ache. After stretching, I realize that I'm no longer hooked up to the IV. Yay.

"What're you doing here?" I ask, looking around the room for Logan. "Where's Logan?"

"I'm your chariot, milady," Blake says with a bow. "As for Logan, he's in your theater room with the others. Everyone's here now, only waiting for you."

"I need to brush my teeth first."

Blake leans down and scoops me up in his arms. I squeal in alarm.

"I can walk! I can walk."

"Actually, you can't, not yet." He laughs when I give him a pouty face. "Doctor's orders. No exertion until Dr. Hayes has cleared you."

"Put me down," I say as indignantly as I can manage through a grin. "You are not going into the bathroom with me."

"Hurry up, breakfast is waiting."

"Pancakes?"

"Maybe."

I walk into the bathroom and shut the door, leaning my forehead against it to catch my breath. How can my body still be so exhausted? When I turn around to head to the counter, I smile and my heart melts just a bit. My brother left clothes in here for me to change into. I toss aside my nightshirt covered in tigers and slip Gavin's *Theory of a Deadman* t-shirt over my head. It falls to my thighs which actually looks cute with my favorite leopard-print leggings folded up with it. I huff and puff while pulling the leggings on, falling against the counter when I'm done. Maybe it's a good thing I have a were-wolf lackey this morning. After brushing my teeth and running a brush through my wild hair, I decide that I'm as presentable as I'll be today.

"Ready?" Blake asks when I return.

I nod, and he sweeps me off my feet into his arms. He carries me to the theater room, where our friends are gathered talking over one another. Typical Circle meeting. Rebecca's voice carries over the others as she lectures Carl about shadow people. Raven and Daniel are huddled together in the corner whispering. Perhaps they bonded last night while she protected him. I don't miss the jealous look that crosses Blake's face for a brief moment when he sees them. He hides it behind a bright smile as he sets me on the sofa beside Logan.

"Morning," Logan says before stuffing a bite of pancake drenched in syrup in my mouth.

I savor the syrup-soaked sweetness. "Now that's something worth getting up for." I glance at him, taking in his unharmed appearance. "You seem to be in one piece. I guess Dad never discovered you in my room last night."

"Yeah, not so much," Logan says through a grimace. "Dr. Hayes came in this morning around five to check on you and remove your IV. She must've said something to your dad because he showed up right after she left. He came in all pissed, but the moment he saw how peaceful you were, sleeping soundly in my arms, he sighed, scrubbed his hand over his face, and backed out of the room."

"It's not like we were really sneaking or anything… Gavin left the door open."

Logan chuckles. "Yes, and you're dad is always so reasonable when it comes to boys in your room."

Dad appears in the doorway like he heard us talking about him or something, but he has a plate in his hands. He sets it down on my lap, and I have to fight wiggling in happiness. Chocolate chip pancakes covered in maple syrup. Man, life doesn't get much better than this!

"Thanks, Dad," I say before cutting off a large piece and devouring it. "Sorry about Logan and breaking the rules."

"You slept peacefully last night. No nightmares." Dad rubs the back of his neck with his hand. "Besides, Gavin admitted to being the guilty party. He couldn't stomach another scream."

I hang my head. "I'm sorry I kept you up two nights in a row."

"What, no!" Dad sits on the arm of the sofa and kisses my head. "I'm relieved you finally slept in peace last night. Hearing you cry out in the middle of the night was torture. Logan is always welcome here, with my permission." He pauses and looks at the door. "Or Gavin's. No closed doors, though."

"No closed doors," I repeat, studying my plate to hide the bright flush spreading across my cheeks.

"Bed rest until Tammy has a chance to check you over." He smooths my hair back, ruffling the top of my head like he did when I was little.

"I can walk, you know."

"Not until you're cleared." He pauses and gives me stern eyes. "Promise."

"Promise. By the way, where is Dr. Hayes?" I'm betting Dr. Tammy Hayes is curled up in Dad's bed. I still haven't quite adjusted to the… uh… intimate side of their relationship.

"In the shower," Dad says like it's the most normal thing in the world. Eww, and weird in my book. But

Dad's really happy, and I suppose that's all that matters. "She'll be in shortly."

"Hey, Cici." Daniel plops down on the sofa arm the moment Dad vacates it. "Good to see you up and about."

"I need to get out of here. I'm bored out of my mind!"

"Yeah, well 'out of here' is school. It's Tuesday."

My mind immediately goes into panic mode. "Oh, no! I missed the chemistry test."

Daniel sighs and does a fake face-palm. "No, it's, 'yay, I missed the chemistry test'."

"You got an exemption for the test," Rebecca says, leaning over the back of the sofa. "Showed Mr. Martinez your notes. He was impressed."

"How did you get into my locker?"

"I've been working on my B&E skills." She says it like it's an accomplishment to be proud of... criminal activity. "You never know when we'll need to break in somewhere for an investigation."

"And I'm sure Mr. Kincaid sanctioned this," Logan says with a snicker.

"Raven's dad did."

I glance over at Raven who is leaning against the wall talking to Blake. Her dad is a higher-up in the Circle, and it's common knowledge that he has unorthodox tactics. I heard that he's put Raven in danger more than once in pursuit of the vampires who killed her mother. It's been a sore spot with Blake since he got here.

"No, starshine, just no," Blake says, his hands clenched in fists at his side. "I can't let—"

"Shh," Raven hisses. "Not here."

"This isn't over." Blake bangs his fist on the wall before storming across the room.

"Well, on that note," Rebecca says, making a big show of opening her laptop and organizing some papers. "Let's get to the wrap up. Mr. Kincaid only cleared us through third period today. We need to get the case notes done. Kacie, we'd like to add your, uh, experiences to the file. Unless it's too…"

"No, I can do this."

Logan takes my plate, leaving me to fidget by wringing my fingers. When Daniel places his hand on mine to stop my nervous movements, I grab onto the lifeline.

"Hey, it's good to see you breathing," I say, squeezing his hand.

"It's good to be breathing." Daniel stares at me with a slight smirk, letting me know he's well aware of my deflection.

"No problems?"

"Not even a whisper of anything paranormal," Raven says with a frown. "I missed all the action to babysit him, and he was never in any danger."

"Yeah, about that…" I trail off searching for the right words. Daniel needs to know, but it's going to upset him. "Tracy had no intention of killing anyone. I was in her head, I mean she was in mine."

"For someone who didn't want to hurt us, she and her cronies managed to do a lot of damage," Logan says, holding up his broken fingers.

"They were throwing tantrums." I take several even breaths, hating that I have to tell one of my best friends such awful news. "I don't think the threat to Daniel was Tracy. I think Logan's premonition was of something else still to happen."

"Crap." Daniel jumps off the arm of the sofa, backing away from me like I'm the danger to him. "Crap."

"I'm so sorry," I say, holding my hand out to him.

He takes it and returns to his perch beside me. "It's okay, Cici, really. I need to know."

"We *will* figure this out, Daniel," Rebecca says, her eyes downcast. "I promise."

Daniel nods. "I know we will. Let's move on, wrap this up."

Guess that's my cue. I take a deep breath and let it out in a ragged sigh. Maybe sharing will help ease the nightmares. I doubt Dad will let Logan sleep over indefinitely.

"Tracy was keeping a pretty big secret from her friends. It was all in a journal we found under her mattress which I... well, she in my body, burned. When she possessed me, I got lots of her memories, emotions, relived her death."

Logan wraps his arms around me, and I fall against him, snuggling into his warmth. Gritty, awful images flicker through my mind, remnants of Tracy that won't go away. Closing my eyes, I lean my head on Logan's shoulder and bite my lip to keep from crying out. My nose burns. Tears will soon follow if I can't stop the horror movie in my head.

"Let's focus on something else," Rebecca says, pulling me from the nightmare images. "Do you know where they went? Between the first cleansing and their return. Was it Purgatory?"

"I have glimpses, images only... you have to understand it's all so hard to..." I trail off, trying to focus on the time before their arrival. "I see gray, like fog or lots of clouds. Dark figures. I don't see any faces, but I know there are others there. It's like a gray desert. Rocks. Crags. Endless as far as I can see. I feel despair. Awful, gut-wrenching anguish. Time doesn't move forward here. There's no escape. No hope—"

"Stop!" Logan's shout brings me back.

I cling to him, shaking from the overwhelming emotions still coursing through me. Without a word, Raven holds a tissue to my nose, and I realize it's bleeding. Taking the tissue, I lean my head back to stop the flow. Psychic overload. The room spins. I close my eyes, but now I feel like I'm on a ship. My eyes fly open, and I stare at the white ceiling, waiting for it to stop moving.

Rebecca's face appears above me, concern radiating in her eyes. "Look, I think we have enough for the report. You don't need to do this."

Though I want to take the out offered so badly, I can't.

"No, let's do this. Maybe the images will fade once I've shared Tracy's secret." I pause, trying to organize my thoughts, but everything is still a jumbled mess. "She had a psychic gift. Tracy could read thoughts in life and death, but only negative ones."

Logan groans. "Well that's one mystery solved."

"And I thought my power was bad," Daniel says, staring at his hands.

"Why couldn't she read the professor's intentions?" Rebecca asks. "She should have seen his evilness from a mile away."

I slump a bit as I remember the utter joy she felt at meeting someone she couldn't read. "She couldn't read him and was ecstatic about it. It was so sad…" I trail off, unable to continue as Tracy's leftover emotions overwhelm me once again. All of her feelings about Jeffrey rush forth in an emotional tsunami: admiration, love, curiosity, dread, anger, fear. They batter me relentlessly, pulling at me, begging my understanding. "I-I'm sorry. I don't—"

"Let me help," Blake says as he leans against the wall, his arms crossed over his chest. His posture doesn't look helpful at all, but I can't tell if he's angry or upset. "I overheard your conversation with Tracy Saturday night. Basically she was in love with Professor Evil and was in on his plotting. I heard her say, 'it was supposed to be Angela.' I'm guessing that dick used both girls. He enjoyed playing on their fears. What I don't know is whether Tracy knew what he planned to do."

"She didn't. Not completely." I let out a pained groan and rub my head. Sorting through the myriad of confusing feelings and memory pieces I experienced while merged with Tracy's spirit is difficult at best. Everything is jumbled, strange. "He had the same plan with Tracy that Angela described to us. Experiment with LSD and other drugs in an effort to secure our country's supremacy. His words not mine."

"I've done more research on the MKUltra experiments. There's not a lot out there that hasn't been redacted." Rebecca stares at the ceiling and blows her bangs from her face. "It kind of struck a chord. I mean Angela, she reminded me so much of myself. I can understand young, naïve girls falling for such a scam. They would view the professor as an authority figure. It was a different time. I'm making excuses."

Carl wraps his arm around her, drawing her into a brief hug. "No, you're right. It was different back then. What happened to Angela, I can't see that happening to you. You only see her academic side. But that's only part of a person. Angela was fresh-faced, innocent, um… no street-smarts. Not you. I could see you setting up and exposing the professor for the rat he is but never falling for it."

"Oh, Carl." Rebecca leans against him, slapping his shoulder. "When did you get so smart?"

Carl's mouth opens and closes a few times, but no words emerge. A red flush creeps over his cheeks.

"So the creepy professor got additional kicks playing Angela and Tracy off of each other," Blake says coming to Carl's rescue.

"Why did he choose to spare Angela?" Logan asks.

Rebecca sits back up. "Was she spared or was she the ultimate victim?"

The others gape at her, but I know exactly what she means. "To a manipulative bastard like the professor, long-term emotional torment is more of a high than a one-time murder, no matter how bloody that murder is."

Rebecca nods. "Angela was the picture of innocence. From a small town, sweet, naïve, the first in her family to even dream of attending college. To take that rosy outlook and completely destroy it... I think that would be the ultimate high for someone like Dr. Rosenthal. She was at the trial every single day until her breakdown. She testified, she cried, she broke. He got to relive that night whenever he saw her."

"That's sick!" Raven says, her fists up as though she can fight the long-dead professor.

"Salt and iron for ghosts, not fists," Blake says. Raven sticks her tongue out at him and he laughs. "Maybe later."

"In your dreams!"

"Every night, starshine, every night."

"Excuse me," Rebecca says, clearing her throat several times. "Let's finish the meeting before you two fight each other."

"How is Angela? Have you talked to her?" I ask.

"She's coping, alone." Rebecca gives me a solemn look. "She needs support so Mrs. Finley is trying to convince her to join a coven near her." She brightens. "On a positive note, we're heading to an all-doodle rescue near Austin this weekend. All poodle mixes in need of good homes."

"I still feel guilty for taking her familiars," Logan says with a frown. "Doesn't seem right."

"Familiars pick us, not the other way around. Do you think I'd have crows following me everywhere if there was a choice involved? At least you can leave the cats at home."

Logan shakes his head. "I think they were cat burglars in a previous life. They keep breaking out of the house and stuff is going missing."

"If it makes you feel any better, Angela told me they always creeped her out and was rather relieved they were gone. She's a dog person." Rebecca pauses, clicking through a few different screens on her laptop. "What's the status of the spirit board?"

"Burned and the ashes scattered in the Hill Country and in two different bodies of water," Daniel says. "One less board to worry about."

Rebecca nods and makes a couple notes. "Great! Thanks for handling that, Daniel. Carl, how is everything going at the sorority house?"

"So, yesterday I went down there to go through the house records. We wanted to know why the sorority boarded up the room and plastered over it rather than cleaning it. I mean, it's not just me, it's weird right? Well, it wasn't laziness or disgust. The seventies were a weird time all right. The house mother was a spiritualist who thought that the spirits would never rest in peace if the scene was tampered with. So after the police finished their investigation, the room was boarded up and forgotten."

"That worked just great," Logan mumbles, shaking his head. "It may have helped tie them here."

"How?" Rebecca asks.

"Cleaning, changing, moving forward all equal moving on with life. That's why spirits can become so enraged when renovations are done. It wakes energy and stirs things up. But it also reminds the spirits that they are just that, spirits, dead and gone. By keeping everything intact, they froze a moment in time, and I think it was a constant beacon for the three ghosts."

"Interesting theory, Logan," Rebecca says, her fingers flying over her laptop keys as she enters her notes. "We need to research it more. I think that's everything I need for now. Time to head to school."

Daniel groans. "Do you have to sound so damned cheerful about it?"

"I'll let that slide, given your current circumstances," Rebecca says, patting his shoulder.

"Don't remind me…"

I sit quietly while everyone files out of the room, listening to the easy banter. Once they're gone, I lean against Logan and consider taking a nap. He wraps his arm around my shoulders, and I rest my head against his chest, listening to the steady beat of his heart.

"Should we call Dr. Hayes or your dad?" Logan asks. His voice rumbles in his chest, waking me from a pleasant doze.

Yawning, I stretch and then wrap my arms around him, hugging his waist. "Why bother. They'll find us sooner or later. And I haven't been released from bed rest yet. Let's just stay quiet and hope they forget about us for a while."

He lays his cheek on the top of my head. "Sounds like a plan."

The End

Thank you for reading *Twisted Sisters*! If you enjoyed this story, please consider leaving a review on Amazon. Reviews are very important, especially for a newer author. It doesn't have to be long. Short and sweet reviews are wonderful too.

I love communicating with my readers. Please feel free to send me an email if you have any questions or would like to discuss the world of books.

www.kimberleighwheaton.com

@Cymberle

www.facebook.com/KimberLeighWheaton

cymberle1@gmail.com

About the Author

Kimber Leigh Wheaton is a bestselling YA author with a soft spot for sweet romance. In addition to writing, she works as an editor for two publishers, as well as select indie authors. She is married to her soul mate, has a teenage son, and shares her home with three dogs and lots of dragons. Kimber Leigh is addicted to romance, video games, super-heroes, villains, and chocolate—not necessarily in that order.

(If she has to choose, she'll take a chocolate covered super-hero!)

Winner of the 2014 Rising Star Award at the BTS Red Carpet Awards in NOLA & a Silver Medal for YA Mystery/Horror in the 2015 Moonbeam Children's Book Awards.

Acknowledgements

~

While writing can be a very solitary pursuit, there are many people involved in the production of a book. *Twisted Sisters* was a long time in coming. In fact, I want to thank Myra Nour with BTS Book Review Magazine for helping me find my way back to writing after several months of severe writer's block. When I won the 2014 Rising Star award at the Red Carpet Awards, it inspired me to write again, and I picked up *Twisted Sisters* where I left off earlier in the year.

I met lots of great authors when I went to ARC in NOLA for the convention and awards ceremony. In those four days, I learned how important it is for a writer to interact with readers and other writers. Going solo is lonely, confusing, and really hard. I learned an important lesson and am stronger for it.

I want to thank my cover artist, Amanda Matthews, who has become a writing friend over the last year. Her covers are amazing, as is her writing. Thanks to my beta readers, proofreader, and formatter. The book would be an ugly mess without you all.

And a special thanks to my family for their continued support. This business is filled with lots of ups and downs—sometimes within days of each other. There are times when I wonder why I keep writing, why I put myself out there when I am so shy and sensitive. But then the next story hits, and off I go. Writing is a passion, a driving need. I'm beginning to think it isn't a choice at all.

And lastly, thanks to my readers. I love you all!

The Orion Circle Book 1
Tortured Souls

Winner:

2015 Silver Medal for YA Mystery/Horror in the
Moonbeam Children's Book Awards

2014 Rising Star and Best Cover in the
BTS Book Review Magazine
Red Carpet Awards

Sometimes Rest in Peace isn't an option

Kacie Ramsey sees ghosts—and it's ruining her life. Her mother left, her father blames her, and no matter how hard she tries, she can't keep the ghosts away. Now a new power has emerged. Nightly visions of grisly murders and a relentless predator draw her to the brink of insanity.

When the phantom appears at a party, Kacie's longtime crush, Logan, saves her. He invites her to join the Orion Circle, a group of supernatural hunters with chapters in schools all over the country. Through the Circle, Kacie learns to embrace her spiritual powers, and for the first time in her life she feels in control rather than a victim.

But the Foxblood Demon will not give up so easily. A demented serial killer in life who trapped the souls of the thirteen children he murdered, imprisoning them within the walls of his mansion. Now in death, he plots his return while drawing power from the pure souls of the children. He recognizes something in Kacie he's never seen before—a medium powerful enough to provide a vessel for his tainted soul.

Kacie can't ignore the tortured souls of the children crying out to her every night. With Logan at her side, she will fight the Foxblood Demon. But can they banish this powerful phantom, or will Kacie lose not only her body, but her eternal soul to the monster?

Light Chronicles Book 1
Shadow Fire

YA Romantic Fantasy
Clean Reads

Ashlyn – a free-spirited teenager whose peaceful life is shattered when the village elders honor her with a perilous quest to recover a stolen relic.

Zane – a jaded mercenary, torn by his undeniable desire for Ashlyn and the dark secret that could make her hate him forever.

Delistaire – a malevolent sorcerer driven by an insatiable lust for power.

All three are bound together by an ancient relic supposedly infused with the power of a Goddess.

Shadow Fire – adventure, passion, secrets, and betrayal

As Ashlyn and Zane race to stay one step ahead of the evil lurking in the shadows, their passions are ignited and their bond strengthens. But will they find the relic before Delistaire? Or has their entire quest been orchestrated from the very beginning by a madman in pursuit of ultimate power?

Each installment of the *Light Chronicles* is a standalone story.